HARRIET SCOTT CHESSMAN

THE LOST SKETCHBOOK OF EDGAR DEGAS

Outpost19 | San Francisco
outpost19.com

Copyright 2017 by Harriet Scott Chessman.
Published 2017 by Outpost19.
All rights reserved.

Chessman, Harriet Scott
     The Lost Sketchbook of Edgar Degas/ Harriet Scott Chessman
     ISBN 9781944853136 (pbk)

Library of Congress Control Number: 2016916440

This is a work of fiction. Names, characters, places, and incidents are informed by historical events but are the product of the author's imagination or are used fictitiously here. According to historical records, Estelle's move took place several months earlier than noted here, the household staff has been extrapolated from common practices of the era, and Edgar Degas' state of mind is speculation based on biographical studies.

OUTPOST19

ORIGINAL
PROVOCATIVE
READING

Advance acclaim for Harriet Scott Chessman's
The Lost Sketchbook of Edgar Degas

"Harriet Scott Chessman has once again invented an utterly beguiling story inspired by art. This time, in her novel inspired by a Degas sketchbook that may have once existed, she has given us a richly evocative and emotionally true portrait of Edgar Degas during his 1872 visit among his Creole cousins in New Orleans. With the clarity and simplicity of a piano sonata, *The Lost Sketchbook of Edgar Degas* is a novel about perception, enduring love, and the complex family legacy of a great artist."
— Katharine Weber, author of *The Music Lesson*

"A beautiful meditation on the interplay of art, time, and memory, that is itself a luminous portrait of a woman without vision who is just beginning to see."
— Ann Packer, author of *The Children's Crusade* and *Swim Back to Me*

"Few writers would have the courage to tell a story of one of the most famous male visual artists of all time through a blind female narrator. Harriet Scott Chessman does it with simple grace in *The Lost Sketchbook of Edgar Degas*, delivering in Estelle Degas' engaging voice — and in astonishingly vivid detail — 1880s New Orleans, the famous artist's lost sketchbook, and the challenges of marriage, family, and love. The result is deeply affecting, and compelling."
— Meg Waite Clayton, *New York Times* bestselling author of *The Race for Paris* and *The Wednesday Sisters*

"In this mesmerizing novel, Harriet Chessman gives us intimate glimpses of a celebrated artist's eloquently human landscape, saturated with the dense complexities of family life in 19th century New Orleans. This nuanced story of love lost and found, wrapped around the experience of seeing and being seen, is itself a masterful work of art."
— Elizabeth Rosner, author of *Electric City* and *Gravity*

Advance acclaim for Harriet Scott Chessman's
The Lost Sketchbook of Edgar Degas

"*The Lost Sketchbook of Edgar Degas* reveals what we see, what we refuse to see, and how beautiful and sad love is either way. Chessman brings us 19th-century New Orleans on one monumental day in which the discovery of a sketchbook leads to the reevaluation of a whole life. This novel is a profound delight from beginning to end."
—Micah Perks, author of *What Becomes Us* and *Pagan Time*

"I read *The Lost Sketchbook of Edgar Degas* with deep admiration for Chessman's empathetic powers. She inhabits this sumptuous world of New Orleans with grace and a kind of heightened sensual alertness, a mystery that unravels level by level as Tell, a fetching character, comes through the oblique sketchbook of her gifted cousin to an awareness of herself, her world, her family—a reality that has become 'simply history' in the best way: imaginatively conceived and assimilated. This is a lovely novel that I would recommend to anyone."
— Jay Parini, author of *The Last Station*

Praise for Harriet Scott Chessman's
Lydia Cassatt Reading the Morning Paper

"For me, it achieves the sublime."— Susan Vreeland

"Beautifully captures the rich relationship between model and painter and between sisters."— Tracy Chevalier

"Entrancing ... heartbreaking ... Makes [itself] felt long after one has finished the book."— *New York Newsday*

"Chessman has allowed herself to inhabit another's world with grace and humility."— *San Francisco Chronicle*

"One feels the author's magnifying glass over their lives, with its genteel distortions and the enormous eye of the writer."
— *Los Angeles Times Book Review*

Also by
Harriet Scott Chessman

The Beauty of Ordinary Things
Someone Not Really Her Mother
Lydia Cassatt Reading the Morning Paper
Ohio Angels
My Lai (libretto)

To Marissa, Micah, Gabriel, Tom and Elijah

HARRIET SCOTT CHESSMAN | THE LOST SKETCHBOOK OF EDGAR DEGAS

Some of Degas' most beautiful and haunting paintings came out of the winter of 1872–73, when he stayed with his Creole cousins, Didi, Mouche, and Tell, in New Orleans. The sketchbook found by my character Tell—Edgar Degas' cousin and sister-in-law—is a fiction. However, art historians have wondered about the absence of a sketchbook devoted to New Orleans. This is the mystery that has inspired my story.

Ah! My dear friend, what a good thing a family is.

> Degas to Désiré Dihau
> from New Orleans, 11 November 1872

One does nothing here, it lies in the climate, nothing but cotton, one lives for cotton and from cotton. The light is so strong that I have not yet been able to do anything on the river.

> Edgar Degas to Henri Rouart
> from New Orleans, 5 December 1872

A loose leaf torn from the lost sketchbook of Edgar Degas, March 1873

Tomorrow I leave this city of New Orleans. I think I will always dream of how it stretches out in the morning sun like a gigantic sleeping cat, some of its streets washed and clean in sunlight, others foul-smelling and filthy, the wetlands up toward Lake Pontchartrain flatly beautiful, the race horses groomed in their stalls at the Fairgrounds, the docks a hive of sweating movement, the bayous glittering, cotton offices humming, dogs racing through gardens, children playing with toy soldiers, and over gates and fences, lemon trees, orange trees, climbing roses, or weeds as high as windows. Most of all, I shall dream of faces open, clear as light, all colors, shining cream and rose, bronze, ebony, cinnamon, and women holding babies, two women singing in a saffron room, dogged by shadows, one child servant shepherding her charges, one woman of grace and courage, her sight a blank, her love filling the world around her, in spite of all. Such beauty—I could not have known there would be such beauty—and may I hold all of this in my heart, and in my inner eye; may I continue to open my eyes; and may her light always shine inside me, so.

Estelle Musson Balfour Degas
January 5th, 1883
New Orleans

1

I have been unpacking boxes in this new house all morning, hoping to comb through as many as I can. Soon Didi will come over to help, and in the afternoon—astonishing!—Honor Benoit. I haven't seen Honor in ten years, since the winter Cousin Edgar came to live with us here in New Orleans. I remember her as a slender colored girl, playing with Josie in our back garden, carrying buckets of orange peels and lettuce leaves to the compost pile, holding my Odile on her narrow hip, picking bugs from the tomato plants, standing on an overturned bucket to help her aunt Lily knead bread dough, or hang up blouses and baby blankets on the clothesline. She came to us before I lost my sight, so I can see her as clear as day. Of course, she will be a young woman now.

I was just telling Didi yesterday, I miss our old house, up toward Lake Pontchartrain. Papa did not own it—none of us owned it—yet it was a beautiful structure, large and welcoming, big enough to hold Papa, Didi, Mouche's family and my own, the servants, all of us. And when Edgar lived with us for those five months, it was just about big enough for him as well.

"I miss it too, Tell," Didi said, as she hemmed Odile's dress for me. "It was a lot of house to keep orderly, though."

"Oh, yes. As soon as one room was clean, the children would blow through like a hurricane."

"And the dog," my sister said wryly. "Don't forget the dog."

Ah, the dog. Vasco da Gama—one of Cousin Edgar's whimsies, that name. A pure mutt and stray, yet once he came sniffing around that winter and Edgar fed him, the hound took it upon himself to become our protector. The children loved him. My sisters said he slept with one eye open on the front porch or the back stoop. You could hear him barking whenever a stranger came through the gate. Yet he'd let our children pull his ears and put hats on him. I liked to scratch him behind his scruffy, faithful ears.

I wish I could know how that house looks now, how New Orleans looks. Sometimes I go over and over the pictures in my memory, so as to make sure I still have them, a whole bunch, bright and almost clear.

Our magnolia stood gracefully in one corner of the front garden. Climbing roses spilled over portions of the iron railing protecting the yard. In one corner of the garden, the grass was uncut, profuse, and sometimes filled with wildflowers, just as I liked it. Across the wide avenue, white or cream-colored houses sat placidly, cousins to ours. On fine days, I would walk along Esplanade Avenue with my sisters and our children, accompanied by Honor or another servant. My lovely sister Mouche would laugh about something comical, and tuck a strand of hair behind her ear.

By the time Edgar came to visit us in New Orleans, I could barely see the house at all, or the magnolia, or the lemon tree, or the toys scattered throughout the house, or the saffron rooms, the baby grand piano René had bought for me in Paris. I couldn't see Lily or our gardener

Augustus. I couldn't see Honor or the maids. I couldn't see Mouche or Didi, or Papa, or my three children, or Mouche's children, or our iridescent parrot. I couldn't see my pregnant self in the mirror.

My world was almost, by then, erased from my sight as thoroughly as with an India rubber. I could see some light, in the periphery, and hazy suggestions of objects, yet all of it had become mostly clouds. I would give much now, just to see those touches of blurred light still.

Odile—a year old then—was the first of my children I hadn't been able to see well, from birth. I *felt* I could, though; I felt that I could just about see her face. I am so lucky—God knows I am—that she is still with me now. It is important to struggle each day to hold to the present, and to be glad for what is here. Odile and Gaston help me in this effort. Children do buoy you up, if you let them. You can't just sink under. You have to be here for them, thinking about clothes and lunch and the little details of each day. "Here I am!" I sometimes feel I'm saying to the world, or to God. "Here I am, still."

Odile said at breakfast this morning, "This house looks like a big wedding cake. It looks like a dream." She's enchanted with the pineapple medallions on the ceilings, and the cherry banister curving to the second floor. She loves the marble mantels too—a pink-gray color, luscious-sounding. "Touch this, Maman!" my spirited daughter says, as she brings my hand along one of the cool surfaces.

Soon we will unpack candles to go on the mantels, and Didi will help me decide which paintings to place above. I'm sure she'll say something, as usual, about her wish to have one—just one!—of Edgar's paintings from his visit.

He made so many, and then he brought all the dry canvases back with him, with instructions on how to pack the wetter ones, once they'd dried. "Think of all those portraits of you and Mouche, Tell!" Didi said around Christmas, as we started to bring our modest watercolors and landscapes down from our cottage walls, to prepare them for this move. I agree with her, yet what can be done? The paintings were Edgar's, to do with as he wanted, even if they were of our household. The one I most wish we could have is the one of the children sitting together on the doorstep, in view of our back garden, Vasco da Gama planted staunchly nearby. I asked Mouche and Didi to describe that one to me in great detail, more than once, so that I could picture it, hold onto it, in my mind's eye.

Our cook Hattie says the kitchen is just fine, the sinks a good porcelain, the spot for a vegetable garden by the back door sunny. It's noisier on this southern portion of Esplanade Avenue. There's a constant rattle of carriages here. I like this, in a way. It's reassuring to feel a neighborhood bustling—maybe it distracts me in just the way I need. And once Didi and Papa join us, in a few days, this house will surely feel full to bursting. After so much has happened, it is important to have hope.

•

As soon as Edgar arrived in New Orleans in the warm season just before *la Toussaint*, I felt him struggling with something, trying to recover from—well, I didn't know what. The Prussian War, I thought, because he had bravely volunteered as an officer, to help defend Paris from the

Germans circling round. We had read about the wintry siege of Paris in the papers, frightened to learn how desperate the Parisians had become, so starving that they ate cats, horses, dogs, even circus animals. All Edgar would tell us was that he began to lose his sight during that siege. He thought it was due to the cannons firing so close to his head. This was possible, yet I thought otherwise. It was clear to me that he had the same condition I had— the blank spot at the center of his eyesight, growing and growing, until only the barest light would remain on the periphery, and then, at last, nothing. I didn't say this to him. Yet I think he couldn't bear sometimes to look at me, and to realize in my face his own possible future. His eyes meant the world to him.

Edgar's visit was almost a complete surprise. René had been doing business for months in Europe, and all we knew was that he was at long last coming home to me and to our children. A few days before his arrival by train from New York, he sent a telegram to say his brother Edgar was with him. Our family was stunned at first—Edgar here! where would he sleep? how would he adjust to our domestic life? how would our food suit him?—and then cautiously happy. For the first time in Edgar's life, we realized, he would be visiting the country and city of his mother's girlhood, where René and I had married and begun our family. "I am half American, you know," Edgar had often said to us, and now he would be seeing the substance of this claim. Often, when I'd lived in France during our Civil War, Edgar had asked me to describe New Orleans, and I'd done my best. Now here he would be, to see it for himself. I hoped he would find something in it to love, even though it was still so raggedy from the War. Maybe he would admire it so much, he would decide to live here, as René had. I wished our opera were open. I knew Edgar loved opera. I hoped we could at least entertain him in our own way, with songs and piano.

On the day of their arrival, the outdoor platform bristled with the noise of carts and people. My children hadn't seen their Papa for half a year. Odile hadn't even been walking when René left, and now you had to keep ahold of her or she'd be toddling off to who knows where, a little goose. Pierre had grown into a sturdy two-year-old in a new sailor suit who'd been asking question after question about whether his Papa had a mustache and a hat, and where his Papa had been, and how big the train would be, and had the train come all the way from France.

Josie was ten, and I sensed her jumble of emotions. To her, René was the Frenchman I'd married when she was a little girl. She had been born just three weeks after my young, brave Joseph perished on the battlefield in Corinth, Mississippi, and she had been my only child for many years, before I married René. It had, in truth, taken René a while to adjust to fatherhood, and Josie had not warmed to him. While he was in Paris summer and fall, Josie had enjoyed having me more to herself, just as she had when she was small. Often, she slipped into my bed in the early hours of the morning—something René would never allow—and wrapped her arms around me, her head snuggled into her favorite spot on my shoulder. Sometimes she patted my big belly through my nightgown, and talked to the baby inside, told it about our house, our parrot, all the family members it would meet once it was born.

Now, as I held Odile on the crowded platform, Pierre clutching my dress and Josie hovering at my elbow, the baby doing somersaults inside me, I was caught up in a big, ardent hug from behind.

"Tell," René said, kissing my neck as he moved his hands to my belly, to feel the baby. I caught the fragrance of his cologne, as he said, "I thought we'd never arrive."

He lifted Odile out of my arms, right over my shoulder, and I could tell he must be tickling her by the way she laughed.

"And where is my boy, then? Where is Pierre?"

"Here I am," said Pierre stoutly.

It was then, in the midst of the jostling, chatty crowd, that my cousin Edgar took my hand and squeezed it warmly.

"*Bonjour, ma chère Estelle.*"

After a second's hesitation, he kissed me on both cheeks. I could feel the softness of his mustache and beard. He smelled of clean clothes and peppermint, with a hint of cigarettes.

"Edgar," I said, my hands held tightly in his.

I ached to see Edgar's face. I would have to ask Mouche and Didi later: did he have scattered bits of silver in his hair, or maybe a whole head of white? Could he really be just about forty? An old man, practically, and I was a mother of such a big brood, at twenty-nine.

"You—," he started to say, brushing my cheek gently, hesitantly, with his hand.

"Yes," I said, my face hot, because I knew what he meant: *it's true, then; you are nearly blind.*

"*Ne t'inquiète pas,*" I said, as lightly as I could. "Don't worry."

Maybe I was the one struck with shyness in front of Edgar in that moment, more than the other way around. I hated to let him see the condition of my eyes. I couldn't think what more to say, and it seemed that he couldn't either. Yet here he was, having come thousands of miles from France, across a whole ocean and half a continent, to be our guest. I rallied myself, and called to the children to welcome our dear cousin.

•

As I fold Josie's silk blouses today—I think they're the ones I had Madame Claire sew for her eighteenth birthday—I listen to Odile and Gaston talking excitedly about something in the postage stamp of a front garden. The filigreed iron fence is so close to the house, only seven steps from the bottom stair. It would be best, and safest, if they would play more often in the back—I'll talk to them soon. Odile has a good head on her shoulders now—after all, she is already eleven—but Gaston is still a little boy, full of beans. If Pierre were still here with us, he and Gaston would be two peas in a pod, in spite of the distance in age and height. I worry that Gaston will open the gate one day and go adventuring by the river, talking to the Irish fishermen or the black men hauling bales of cotton, getting himself crushed by a trolley.

Cousin Edgar has never met Gaston, who was born well after his visit, and he did not meet baby Henri either. But it cheers me to remember that Edgar did know Josie, Pierre, and Odile, and then baby Jeanne, that winter.

When Edgar put Odile into his painting of the children on the doorstep, Mouche said you could see her face much better in that picture than you could see the other children's. She said Edgar had posed Josie to stand in the doorway, holding her hoop as she looked down, her face in the shade of an over-sized bonnet. Pierre's face, Mouche said, was blurry, like the smudge on one's forehead at Ash Wednesday. Honor was in that painting too, although her face was indistinct—my sister described her as a silhouette trying to emerge out of a brown ink spot. Mouche's daughter Carrie sat on the top step, facing away in her white dress, only the smallest sliver of her face visible. And there was Odile—by contrast, strikingly clear. She sat cross-legged, my sister said, her hair fine as a gosling's, her eyes bright and curious, her face tipped to one side as she looked straight out at you.

"I declare, I wish Edgar would show *all* the children to be healthy and lovely as he shows Odile to be," Mouche said. "What is the use of making a portrait if you can't even see the faces?"

"And the garden!" Didi said. "You'd think Augustus had done nothing in it, by the way Edgar paints it, all sandy and brown and dull. He didn't even put in the lemon tree, or the winter roses."

I nodded sympathetically. Mouche's children were her pride and joy, as the roses were for Didi. I agreed that Edgar could have been more diplomatic. I took their complaints with a grain of salt, however. My sisters had gifts of their own, but they knew very little about art. And it was more than this, too: I had always intuited something heavy and shadowy in Edgar, which came out in his painting. Even in my childhood, on our first trip to France, I had understood that this alert, sensitive cousin carried sorrow inside him. I had decided it was because his mother died when he was a boy of thirteen. He may have felt he had to be a leader for his younger siblings, a help to his father, in spite of the way his own life had been ravaged.

Or maybe it was more than sorrow. I don't know what it was. It was like a war going on within his breast. And I thought—he can't help putting such things into his art. Maybe Mouche and Didi couldn't see the artistry or the emotions. I felt them, though. I did.

Once Edgar had settled in to our household, in any case, he showed a polite wish to fit in. He was wonderfully patient with the children, and with the somewhat hectic schedule of our meals. He seemed glad for the company of my sisters and me—something I'd been worried about before he came, because I'd gathered that he lived such a bachelor's life in Paris. I wondered why he had not yet married, and whether he ever would.

My sisters told me that Edgar had a sketchbook with him constantly, on walks and as he sat in the shade of a tree in the back garden, or in our house. I wondered if the sketchbook was like a window for him into our family life, or if it was more like a levee, protecting him from the daily flooding of our emotions.

It was one of those sketchbooks that went missing in our house before Edgar sailed to France that spring. On the rainy March day when he was about to catch the train, and then the boat to Havana, he was frantic, opening drawers, looking into each room of our house, rushing upstairs and even out to the garden shed. One of the few letters he wrote to me, once he was home in Paris, was to ask once more if I could please search for that sketchbook, and send it to him. *Il est très important à mes yeux* , he wrote. *I have drawings in it that I cherish. It is more than an ordinary sketchbook. I wrote in it too. J'espère que tu comprends. Je t'embrasse, Edgar.*

Once Edgar began to paint me in New Orleans, I often thought about reminding him of an awful portrait he had done of me, years earlier, in France. He'd posed me in the wild garden of our rented house in Bourg-en-Bresse, on a damp day in winter—soon after our flight from occupied New Orleans. I hadn't been tremendously patient about being painted that day, my feet cold and wet in the grass. I hoped, however, with all my heart, afterward, that I wasn't quite as ugly as he showed me to be. This was the heart of the matter: I still had most of my sight during that French sojourn, yet he made me look blind. He painted my eyes like dark caves, my skin pasty as dough, my lips a cadaver's pale slash. Didi said straight out to Edgar, albeit in a good-humored tone, what a botch he was making of that portrait, and Edgar had been embarrassed and defensive.

"This isn't going to be just a portrait of Tell, though," he'd said. "It's becoming a painting, Didi. It's not even finished. And in any case, sometimes a painting shows you something in a way that's new, don't you agree?"

Didi had shrugged and said, "I think Tell will agree with me that sometimes it's best to see a pretty woman as she is."

"Well," Edgar said, trying to make the best of it, "of course Tell is beautiful. I am sorry if my portrait doesn't capture her beauty."

Edgar had taken that canvas home with him to Paris,

and we'd never seen it again. I hope it isn't on someone's wall now. I hope no one has to see the image of that unhappy face, barely a face. And I certainly hope no one figures out it's supposed to be a portrait of his Creole cousin Estelle Musson Balfour.

In his first weeks in New Orleans, I have to say, Edgar made up honorably for this earlier misstep. I posed for him a few times, and my sisters agreed I looked presentable, in one portrait especially. I stood by the dining table for that one, arranging gladiolas and roses in a large vase. Edgar had bought the flowers himself.

"I am glad," Mouche said, "that Edgar has made an effort to show you as you are. You're in shadows, in this one, but he's shown a little of your grace."

•

If I were to write to Edgar now, what would I say? Where would I start? I never found his missing sketchbook, and although I wrote to him a few times after that winter, I have received a letter from him only once or twice. The distance between us has grown greater—perhaps it will never be bridged. And yet we came close in those five months in our old house. Does he ever think of us now? I hear that he's become increasingly well known as an artist in France. I am glad for him, if that's true. He most certainly devoted himself to his art.

Gaston comes flying in with news of a fossil he's just uncovered in the garden. He thrusts it into my hand, and I feel the rough ridges on it.

"I know I can find more," he says. "I just need a shovel."

He's taken to talking in English recently—a sign of the times, I suppose. Odile still speaks almost only in French with me, although with her friends she speaks a mixture.

"I don't have a shovel right now, *mon cœur*. Maybe *grand-père* Michel could bring us over a small shovel tomorrow."

"I'll use a spoon then."

"What is the rush, Gaston? And also, I hope you're not digging up the flower bed."

He's speechless for a second, so I can tell that's exactly where he's been messing about.

"Can you find a bare spot in the back yard, where you can dig?"

"Yes, ma'am. I'm going to find jewels too."

I ruffle his fine hair; it's long now, and must be in his eyes. I'll have to ask Didi to cut it. Out of anxious habit, I hold my hands to his cheeks for a moment, to feel for fever or moisture, but his skin is cool and smooth.

He slips out of my touch and goes off to the hall. I hear the front door open, and then Gaston calls out, "Isn't Hattie making a King cake?"

"Yes. She'll make it today."

"When?"

"Well, even if she makes it this morning, *mon ami*, you won't be able to eat it 'til tomorrow. That's Epiphany."

"I'm going to win the little king."

He's thinking of the miniature porcelain king, green, blue, and purple, that Edgar gave us that winter in New Orleans. Gaston wasn't even born yet, but it's always been his favorite of our King cake trinkets. I wish Edgar could know that. I promise myself I will write to him one day, at last, whether he thinks of me or not.

"No one can know where the king is hiding, Gaston. It could be that Odile will get it in her piece. Or your cousins."

I sense Gaston looking at me with his keen wish, and I have to smile.

"If the little king is in my piece, I will give it to you. Ça va?"

"Thank you, Maman!"

"Oh, and Gaston!"

"Yes?"

"The piano is arriving this afternoon."

"All right!" he shouts, as the front door slams. I almost call to him, to tell him he forgot the spoon, but I know he'll be back inside in a moment, with some even better news, something else that's caught his eye—a lizard, a skunk, a white cat with one blue eye, one green.

As I rummage about in a fresh box, filled I think with Josie's art work, or maybe Pierre's or Jeanne's, along with brushes and glass vials of ink or paint, I remember how happy I felt, those first few weeks of Edgar's visit, before I gave birth to Jeanne in December. He praised our house, my children, Mouche's children, Didi's embroidery on all our linens. He praised René's business and Papa's cotton office. "I can't believe my little brother is a businessman!" he'd say. He delighted in our garden.

He had harder days too, though, even at the start. A couple of times he got the dysentery, and kept to his room. He could get very gloomy, and then the old gruffness and melancholy would emerge.

"This weather!" he would say, when he felt ill. "How can you bear it? If it's this warm and humid in the weeks before Christmas, what can it possibly be like in the summer?"

More than anything, he worried about his vision. How could he not? The bright sun was too much for him, and even on cloudy days the haze was too intensely light. Mouche said he rubbed his eyes constantly, and sometimes she caught him with his head in his hands, for all his life like a statue of grief.

The best time of day for Edgar was morning, before the sun had risen very high, or late afternoon. He had no hope of painting on the river, he said, or in fact anywhere outdoors. I felt for him, because I knew what it was like to have the shining world go, bit by bit, from your sight.

It was when he painted me that I felt closest to him. Once René and Papa and Mouche's husband William would be at work, and Mouche's baby Willie would have fallen asleep, and Mouche would have put her feet up for a siesta, and Didi would have started in on the bills at Papa's desk, and Lily would be cooking in the kitchen with the windows wide open, and young Honor would be holding a sleeping Odile as Pierre played in the garden, and Vasco da Gama would be stretched out under a bush somewhere, and Josie might be writing in her diary or reading a book near me, then I could at last be free to pose for Edgar. I was touched that he wanted to devote those hours to painting me. Sometimes we spoke of important things, like Maman's Bright's disease, and her sad death, the year before. And sometimes he made me laugh as he told me about his dogs in Paris, and his time on the ship, trying to draw in spite of seasickness. Often we eased into quietness together, for half an hour at a time.

Now, as I come upon christening dresses, tiny silk shoes, and soft cotton bonnets with lace, I feel the salt tears pricking my eyes. I will those tears to hold off. I try to remember more of my conversations with Edgar as he sketched or painted me. I remember bits here and there. It was more a feeling I recall, though, of being looked at very carefully and very slowly, each inch of my face, my body. Of being cherished—maybe that was it.

2

The table clock in the dining room strikes ten o'clock in the morning with its light chimes, and I've just opened a new box. I'm sure to come across a passel of other things valued by Josie and Pierre, Jeanne and little Henri—not that much for Henri, maybe, since he had so many hand-me-downs and such a mercilessly short life. In a new house, anyway, it seems right to try to go through such items. I can't just hold onto them all forever. Maybe Odile and Gaston and their cousins can have use of some clothes or toys. I know I will have to keep a few special things—Pierre's stamp album for one. I hope Gaston will find that absorbing, once he's a bit older.

Didi should be here any minute to lend me her eyes. She's been busy in the cottage we've been renting ever since we moved out of our house. She's selling whatever she can: furniture, prints, even some of Maman's jewelry. She and I decided that it was better to have the money than to hoard every single piece of jewelry. We agreed on the bracelets and brooches we could part with.

Edgar commented a few times that winter on our luxuries, especially the new clothes the children had, and the gifts René brought home to us from Paris: dozens of new songs in sheet music, yards of silk and muslin and lace, napkins and hand woven table cloths, a silver teapot and service, toys for the children, Champagne, pearl buttons, bracelets and necklaces. And of course the piano, which he'd shipped in August.

"My little brother seems to have made quite a success of his business," Edgar said one day, as I posed with the flowers. Josie had just rushed in to show off a bunch of bracelets she'd put on her thin wrists. I could hear them jingling and clicking together. She must have been dancing for Edgar, by the sound of her thumping feet and his applause. He commented on the colorful ribbons in her hair, and said she looked like a duchess. She flew out of the room, I imagined more like a sprite than a duchess, and I laughed with Edgar.

I remember feeling uneasy when he said that, though, about the success of René's business. He may not have meant too much by it. But I actually wasn't sure that René had had sufficient money to buy all those presents, and I knew he'd go out and spend more for Christmas. I wondered whether he had had to use credit. He was already talking about buying a few bottles of imported wine for our new neighbors, Léonce and America Olivier, who had moved in to the modest house behind ours, visible from our back windows. America and I had started to become friends. Her first child Odile was about one and a half, just like our Odile. I had assured René that a tin of shortbread or cocoa would be a fine gift for neighbors, no matter how amiable they were, and we didn't have to go overboard, but René said he liked to go overboard, and in any case he'd noticed that the Oliviers had good taste when it came to wine.

Something I couldn't forget was the way René had lost thousands of dollars when he first came to America, after I had said yes to him but before we'd married. He'd invested, impulsively, in cotton futures. It was a flimsy and reckless investment, as it turned out, like tossing borrowed gold straight into the ocean. René had persuaded his father, my Uncle Auguste, to back him, through the bank he owned in Paris, so our family on both sides of the Atlantic, including Edgar and Papa, got pulled into that mess. The debt haunted us; it changed us; it was a cloud hovering over our lives, shadowing everything. Papa had to sell our house in the Garden District, after the War, and we made do with the rented house on Esplanade, reducing our expenses.

René never paid back that gigantic sum to the bank, and I doubt he ever will. That very winter of Edgar's visit, Uncle Auguste loaned a new amount to us from his bank. I have no idea how much it all added up to. And when Uncle Auguste died a few years ago, the huge debt remained, on Edgar's plate, as I gather. Maybe Edgar has found a way to pay it back by now. He has a kind of honor and sense of family that would compel him to try. Didi tells me that Edgar and his sisters have been having to live very frugally, in the effort to rise out of indebtedness.

I noticed that winter, how Edgar resisted extravagance. His clothes were well-made, Mouche said, and of excellent material, but he appeared content with what he owned. Instead of five pairs of shoes, one or two would do; instead of twenty shirts, a handful, to be kept clean and well pressed, buttons sewn on when necessary.

Maybe in being the oldest child in his family, Edgar had learned how to rely on himself. René had been the baby—just two years old when their mother died—and even as a girl, I realized that he tended to believe others would pick up after him and smooth over his mistakes. He had an abundance of charm, no question. He had energy, warmth, spirit, ardor that could win people over, undo all hesitation as easily as he could undo your clothing once he was sure of you.

•

Odile has just rushed in from outside with some story about a parrot she's glimpsed in a tree on the neutral ground. Edgar thought it was silly to call that green strip in the middle of Esplanade Avenue neutral. "Is there a war, then, to make neutrality necessary?" he said one day over breakfast. He was laughing. "Good heavens. I'd better figure out at once which side I'm on!"

"It's in the magnolia, Maman!" Odile says. "I wish you could see it! It's red and green, just like Persie! Maybe it *is* Persie!"

"How could it possibly be Persie, Odile? She's with *tante* Didi. She'll come live with us in a few days, sure enough."

"Maybe she flew here, though."

"*Non, je ne crois pas.* Now, Odile, help me with some of these things."

As I pull a few pieces of paper from a chest of Josie's stuff, I am aware of a certain relief, in the parrot's temporary absence. Persie—Persephone—is a walking, chortling recorder of our family life, a living archive of chatter. One moment you can hear Josie, saying, *Bonjour, mon bel oiseau,* and the next moment you can hear little Pierre calling, *Viens! Viens vite, Honor!* or Jeanne saying stubbornly, *Mais non! Je ne veux pas!* A whole room of child spirits, wringing my heart.

"Maman, *s'il te plaît*," Odile says now, "let me see if I can catch the parrot's attention. I could give it some food. Maybe it likes slices of carrot."

I hold out my hands and Odile slowly places her warm, soft ones in mine. I wish keenly in this instant that I could see her. This wish—I always try to overcome it, but sometimes I just cannot.

"It's all right," Odile says. "Don't cry."

"Look here," I say, wiping my eyes with the back of one hand, as I hold onto Odile's hand with the other, "Aunt Didi's coming over soon, but I'd like you to look at some of this, see what these are, whether your big sister would have wanted us to keep them."

"*D'accord*, Maman," Odile says dutifully. "I will help you."

Under more blouses, I come upon a slim bunch of paper—rice paper, I think—tied with a ribbon—letters maybe.

"Odile, could you look at these papers and tell me what they are?"

She takes the paper bundle from me, and then I hear a rustling. She's quiet as she reads, until she gives a little laugh.

"This one you should keep. It's a funny letter to Josie from her friend in school."

"Ah! What friend is that?"

"I can't read the handwriting. Charity, I think."

"I never met a friend of hers named Charity."

But Odile is now like a hummingbird, moving on at a great speed.

"Maybe there's a letter from—someone else," she says.

I know she means her father. I feel myself flushing from my chest to my forehead. It would be a miracle if Odile discovered a letter from René. If he couldn't be bothered half the time to send his monthly payments for the children, I doubt he could have bothered to write to them, especially to Josie.

Odile is rushing on. "Here's something," she says. "Hold this, Maman. Open it."

She places a book in my hands—light and rectangular, with thick pages, a good stock.

"There are drawings in it," she says a little breathlessly, as if she has indeed been whirring her wings at great speed.

"Ah! A sketchbook of Josie's. We'll have to keep this, most certainly."

"No, Josie wouldn't have done these drawings. These are . . ."—I sense Odile searching for the right word—"real."

I have an extraordinary sensation, a flock of doves inside my chest, my head.

"Real?" I say, as Odile perches next to me. I can feel her excitement as she breathes right at my shoulder.

"Well, here's a picture of Vasco da Gama, and it's a really good picture. His tongue is hanging out, very silly, just the way it always did—*tu te souviens*, Maman?"

Edgar's missing sketchbook. Could it be? Where has it been?

Odile pokes me. "Do you remember, Maman? Vasco da Gama, his tongue?"

"*Oui, mon chou.* What else do you see?"

I hear Odile shuffling through the pages.

"Here's a picture of Lily! Lily's hanging up laundry!

Only she looks a little younger. Her back isn't so bent. I can tell it's her, though, because of her skin, and the way she wears her hair, up in a tight bun, and the wisps around her face. Look! There's the door to the kitchen, you can just see a little of it."

Odile is as immersed now as if she's on a treasure hunt like the ones René used to do for her birthday; the children would run in a harum-scarum pack, from one clue to the next, each clue in the form of a riddle. *I swing both ways and I'm in need of paint*, one clue would read. "The back gate!" the children would shout. *A noble guard wears this on his neck*. "Vasco da Gama's collar!"

Odile pats me on the leg. "And here's—someone on a ship—a man looking through binoculars. And, oh—here's the view out our back door in our old house. You can see children. A girl in a pretty dress. I think that's cousin Carrie. Is the baby me, I wonder, or someone else? And who is this colored girl? Was she watching us? You can see Vasco da Gama too, with his tongue out again—and —someone else, a girl in a bonnet, standing up. And here's the neighbors' house." Her voice has grown soft. I listen as she turns more pages. "Oh, here's one that might be—." She hesitates. "I'm not sure."

The table clock ticks in the other room. I gather Odile has seen a drawing of René, and I wonder if he is still a glittering, painful absence in her life, or if memory has been kind to her, and he's faded. Gaston was littler when his papa left, and I think misses him much less, if at all. I doubt he even remembers how René would carry him on his shoulders all through the garden, and let him search his pockets for sweets and pennies. I hope Gaston doesn't remember how irritable his father could get with the children, and how sudden and sharp his slaps could be.

Gaston comes inside, tossing us a quick hello as he heads to the kitchen. He always gets hungry by eleven o'clock, and Hattie has been putting a cold biscuit or a slice of bread and cheese out for him, to tide him over 'til lunch.

Odile touches my hand. "I'm going to go look for the parrot again, Maman. Maybe it's come to our yard. Maybe I can catch it."

I try to draw her attention back to the book in my hands. I must know if this is Edgar's.

"Odile, can you tell—do you see any names in this? Is this a sketchbook, then?"

Odile rifles through the pages. "I see lots of words in French. Lists. Some sentences. And sometimes words for colors. I don't see a name, though."

"Could you read a little to me?"

Odile sighs. Her hair has the fragrance, still, of a child's. Hattie washed it yesterday in the kitchen sink, and I combed it out, to Odile's "ouch's." It comforts me now to put my nose to the top of her silky head as she reads, and she lets me do this. She has one foot in childhood still. Didi says Odile's hair has a burnish to it, in the sun. She says it's just like Mouche's was.

Odile starts to read, in French, "'*A poem she taught me—this line is best.*' And then this is in English: 'Love is not love which alters when it'"—Odile pauses, figuring out a word—"'when it alteration finds.'"

I sense her looking at me. "What does that mean?" she asks.

Then she appears to be moving the sketchbook around

so that she can see something better.

"Mm . . ." she says. "Here's another bit. This one's in French: *'How easily things can tear.'*"

She pauses again. "I don't understand. Why would someone write things like that in a sketchbook? Isn't a sketchbook for pictures?" She adds, "I like the pictures, though."

I am aware of holding my breath. I was the one who read this sonnet to Edgar. *A poem she taught me.* Am I this "she," then? I did share his love for poetry.

Love is not love
Which alters when it alteration finds,
Or bends with the remover to remove:
O, no! it is an ever-fixed mark,
That looks on tempests and is never shaken;

•

Odile pats my shoulder. "Maman, what are you thinking?"

"I don't know, Odile." I try to calm my breathing. *How easily things can tear.* "I do believe this was our cousin Edgar's sketchbook. Do you remember him?"

I know Odile is shaking her head. Of course she wouldn't remember him, although he put her fairy-like portrait in the picture with the other children, hunkered down together on the back steps, with Vasco da Gama guarding them, and Honor hovering on the side.

I so yearned, that winter of Edgar's visit, to be able to look at him once more, to see those dark brown eyes of his, slightly hooded, hawk-like, tender or pained. I thought I could understand something if I could see his face. I thought increasingly that I could feel his loneliness.

3

Odile is flying off again. I hear her talking to Hattie now in the kitchen in an insistent tone of voice, most likely trying to get her to leave her washing and go catch the parrot in the magnolia. Hattie's voice is lower and resistant. I'm sure Odile won't be able to budge her. Hattie went to school with the nuns for many years, as a girl, and I doubt she will stay with us long. Maybe she'll leave Louisiana, as Honor did. She's still just in her early twenties.

Edgar said Odile was a very good model, for a one-year-old. One day, though, like an absent-minded uncle, he gave her a handful of *marrons glacés*, which she ate immediately, one after the other, until she got sick. He gave Carrie some too, and Mouche said Carrie's white dress had to come off afterward and go to Lily to be washed, because it had gotten so sticky from the glaze.

Here on my lap is something Edgar held once, and many times, something he opened, often, to record what he saw in our pretty, messy, crowded house. I wonder if Edgar still misses this sketchbook. I wonder what his days are like now. He must have filled dozens, hundreds, more such books since that winter when he was our guest. Had Josie squirreled this one away, even before the day he left? Or did she come upon it after he'd set sail for Havana?

She liked him; that much was certain. "Maman," she said one evening at bedtime, "Cousin Edgar is going to put me in the picture too. I will be the only one standing, he says, right at the open door."

To think that she held onto this sketchbook of Edgar's all those years. My packrat, I used to call her, my magpie. She saved everything: place-cards, birds' nests, a harmonica still in its case, the toy trumpet Edgar gave her when she was a baby in France, cross-stitch projects started and abandoned, sea shells with sand still inside, her father's embroidered handkerchief. As she started to grow up, she saved satin boxes, filled with all kinds of things: her necklaces, invitations to balls, pressed flowers, charm bracelets. Then there were her sketchbooks too, of all sizes and shapes. She became quite proficient, my sisters said, at drawing, and by the time she was seventeen she'd started pen and watercolor.

What devotion helped her keep Edgar's sketchbook secret? Or did she simply forget about it? Did it become just one more object she had wanted to keep safe, among all her other things, and yet had forgotten?

I wish I could hold onto it, in any case. Poor Papa has tried for years to get even one canvas from Edgar—especially the one he did of Mouche on the balcony, which Papa admired—and Edgar has ignored his requests, why, I have no idea. It's as if he has forgotten us all, and yet, that winter, I thought he loved us.

•

"Well," Didi says when she comes over just before lunch, "did Odile tell you, most of these sketches are of you?"

I am startled. "Really? She didn't say that, no."

Didi has her usual fragrance, a mélange of warm,

yeasty bread, rose water, and coffee. She's grown so plump, her bones crack sometimes when she sits or stands. She is well into her forties now. My big sister! How fast life goes—and how quickly dreams of marriage vanished for her. She's kept us all afloat. What would we have done if she'd married? And then if she had had children, what if I had lost her too, in one of her childbirths, as I lost Mouche?

"You're in dozens of these drawings, Tell. Here you are, holding Odile, *toute petite*—nicely done. Here, you're sitting at what looks like the breakfast table, a coffee cup in front of you. Sitting at the piano. Standing in the front garden, in front of the magnolia perhaps."

I hear my sister go through the pages just like Odile, only a touch more carefully.

"You know, Tell, I think I like these better than the paintings he did that winter. You can sense the life in them. They're nicer, really, more—regular. And the ones of you are more beautiful."

I almost tell Didi something Edgar said, about beauty, but I think she might scoff at it. She is not much for overthinking things, as she puts it. One day, as I was posing, holding a gladiola in my right hand and a rose in my left, Edgar said out of the blue, "There are lots of different kinds of beauty, *tu sais*? Some kinds might not look like beauty at all, but its opposite." He added that it was ugliness he preferred above all things.

Ugliness! It was just like Edgar to say such a thing, right as I was standing there in front of him, having taken care with my hair that morning, and having had Mouche shape my fingernails and buff them.

"I'm not talking about conventions of beauty or actual ugliness," he said, as if he could read my face. "I'm talking about something to hold onto, something real, with real flesh and emotion to it, not disguised. I'm talking about the way it can hurt, to bend a certain way, or how someone— even a woman! yes!—perspires in the sun. I'm not talking about ideals, but about the real thing, shining out."

I understood, yet I still wished to know what I looked like to him, in my ninth month of pregnancy, how he saw me. Did I look to be in my late twenties, as I was, or did I look older? Did I look worn out from three children, two of them under the age of three? Had my eyes lost their brightness, my skin its color? Vanity, vanity.

Gaston and Odile sound as if they're making clothespin figures again in the kitchen, getting underfoot, I'm sure. I hear them talking about what colors to use for the hair and the mustaches.

"Funny," Didi says. "Here's a little map of the area around Carondolet Street; addresses of cotton offices; names—ah! The name of a tailor, I recognize. An eye doctor. Did he go to an eye doctor in New Orleans?"

"I don't know. He had a blind spot, I know that. Like mine. You remember, Didi, don't you? He was very worried about it."

"I remember him complaining an awful lot that winter, Tell," Didi says without sympathy. "I can't remember all of his complaints. Stomach aches, headaches, fatigue, dysentery. He'd sleep well into the morning."

"Well, you think eight in the morning is late."

"I do."

She seems to feel a little compunction about talking ill

of our cousin, then, because she says, "Do you think his eyesight has gotten better?"

"I doubt it got better. I don't think it's the kind of thing that does."

"He still paints, though."

"Yes, I gather he still paints."

Didi gives a soft harrumph. As she turns the pages of Edgar's sketchbook, a cart of some sort rattles past the house, with a fellow crying out about rags and old iron. Odile has forgotten about the parrot, I gather. A cat meows; the children must have let in a stray. I know how they'll try to wheedle their way into Hattie giving it milk, and then scraps, and then a bed by the stove.

"He's written quite a bit too, Tell, almost all in French. In ink, very small handwriting."

"On each page?"

Didi seems to be studying the pages. "No, not each one. Sometimes on a blank page facing a sketch. Mostly, though, it's in the white space to the side of a sketch. Sometimes he's written whole sentences along a page's inner edge, up and down."

"Do all artists do that, I wonder?"

"I have no idea. Oh, and here and there he's put words for colors. Maybe for when he uses the sketch toward painting a picture." She adds, "Ah! Here's something interesting: he wrote, *One tries to catch the real, yet how can one be sure of it?*"

"How, indeed," I say, and suddenly my move to this house near the French Quarter, the day's increasing warmth, the surprise of this sketchbook, of these thoughts so private to Edgar, ten years ago, spread open to be read by my sister and heard by me—all of it overwhelms me with a kind of pain I can't quite understand. In spite of his obvious flaws, Edgar had some quality that made me open up to him. I had a bond with him. It may have been largely unspoken, but it was there.

"It's Edgar's, though. We shouldn't be reading it," I say, for I'm realizing now that Didi may indeed come upon something very private, possibly something hurtful. I had thought Edgar would be circumspect, knowing that such a thing could fall into anyone's hands.

Didi closes it with a light thump.

"I agree, Tell. What should we do with it, then?"

"Well, of course I'll send it to him."

"That's very good of you. Not that he's done a thing for us! Well, I'll take it home to wrap it. I can go to the postal office tomorrow."

"No, no. I'll have Hattie help me wrap it. We'll get it off all right."

I think to myself, just to have it nearby for a few days more—that will be something that might almost bring that time back to me, all the best of it: the children, when they were little and healthy; Jeanne's December birth; her christening at St. Rose of Lima, with Edgar standing up as her godfather; my mornings and afternoons by Edgar's side, chatting with him over coffee, or as I posed.

"What time did you say Honor would be coming today?" I ask.

"Two o'clock."

"Josie used to play with her."

"When they were little."

"Honor was just a year older than Josie, think of that.

Remember when they climbed the tree, and we couldn't find them anywhere?"

Didi makes a clucking noise, and I know she's remembering too.

"I was beside myself," I say. "They must have spent hours up there, as quiet as fish. Eluding capture. I walked up and down in the yard, calling for them."

"They brought paper and pencils and books into the branches with them," Didi says. I can imagine her little smile, her crinkly eyes, as she shakes her head over her niece's mischief. "Papa's world atlas too, *tu te souviens?*"

"I thought surely someone had lured them out of the yard."

What had happened, once they'd been discovered? Lily had most likely whipped Honor with a switch on the backs of her bare legs—punishing her niece before we could, as usual, and making sure she did it well enough that we wouldn't feel the need to add our own, yet not so well that Honor would be truly hurt. Honor was the apple of her aunt's eye, any fool could see, as Josie was of mine.

I only rarely punished Josie, though, and I tried to rush to it before René got hold of her. The first time I saw him cut a switch from a bush, she was about seven. We'd just been married, and didn't have our own children yet. Josie had been annoying her stepfather, singing some song or other, as he was trying to talk to me in the evening, when she should have been in bed. "That's enough singing," he said, and I motioned to her to be quiet, but she persisted. He stood up and grabbed her then, and started dragging her into the yard, made her wait beside him while he took out a pocket knife and cut a branch from the witch hazel bush by the kitchen. I followed them out, a fury filling my soul such as I had rarely known before. "You will not touch this child," I said. "Put that switch down this instant." He obeyed me, but not before shaking her arm so hard I thought her head would snap off.

Was I right to intervene, or was I wrong? It's possible I was wrong, in that most likely she needed the discipline, but I couldn't help it—I had to stand up to him. The trouble was, my efforts to protect Josie made René even more irritated with her. She'd been mine for so long, and she had Joseph's forehead and mouth. It was, I suppose, understandable how René felt, but it made one of the earliest tears in our marriage, and although we tried to mend it, I do not think we did.

Edgar had his own childishness. I can't imagine him, though, cutting a switch for any creature; he had a certain kindness that shone out sometimes, toward vulnerable things: horses and dogs and children. I'm not surprised that Josie held onto his sketchbook. That winter of his visit, she hung about near him, as if she'd been a little duckling once, popping out of her eggshell in Bourg-en-Bresse ten years earlier to discover this awkward French duck, who'd bring her treats and draw pictures for her, and here was the duck again, big as life, sitting right smack in her house. Edgar couldn't help being serious and tense, and the other children were often shy around him, but if Josie was afraid, she didn't show it. She was the only one of the children who would hover by his elbow sometimes, watching him draw or paint, and she must have held her breath, to be so quiet that she wouldn't bother him.

To pose, standing against the doorjamb in the big

bonnet and the odd, old-fashioned little shift Edgar had her wear—that was heaven for her. She was fascinated with the way she could be brought into his canvas—she, Joséphine Balfour.

One morning that winter, just before Jeanne was born, Josie said softly to me, "I wish you could see my own paintings, Maman." She caressed my hand as she said this.

"I can see them in here," I said, touching my forehead. "Describe them to me."

•

Over lunch—carrot soup, and flounder sautéed in butter and herbs—Gaston is practically bouncing out of his chair. He can't stop thinking about the King cake Hattie will make, once she clears away the lunch.

"Where is the little king?" he's asking her, as he scrapes his plate. "Do you know where it is, Hattie?"

Hattie says, "I know where it is, Monsieur Gaston. You don't need to trouble yourself about that."

"Maman says I can have it if it's in her piece."

"That's not fair, Gaston," says Odile. "If the king is in Maman's piece, then it's hers. That's the rule."

"Well, she promised me."

"Maybe we should put two trinkets in the cake this year, Hattie," I say.

Hattie holds her own counsel, and I can just picture her giving a shake to her head that is both yes and no, and neither.

"Gaston, you're so tiring," says Odile, in her oldest voice, as if she has a dozen children and Gaston is the worst of them all.

After lunch, Didi is helping me go through table linens. Hattie is in the kitchen, making the dough for the King cake to the accompanying chatter of Gaston. I haven't raised the issue of Edgar's sketchbook again with Didi, although I picture it in the parlor, holding onto all those images, all that life. In the midst of sorting through the linens and then children's blankets, Didi appears to have forgotten all about Edgar.

4

As soon as my sister has walked out the front door carrying two bags full of items to give to the nuns, I find Edgar's sketchbook again on the sofa, and I'm about to open it, just to touch the pages, when I hear someone coming up the back steps outside the kitchen. I hear the door opening, and then I listen to Hattie greeting Honor and to Honor's light, quick walk as she comes through the dining room and into the parlor.

If Josie would be twenty now, how old is Honor? Twenty-one? She has a fragrance that's crisp, like cider and grapefruit, and cotton freshly ironed. Leather soles to her shoes, I can tell. Her bracelets ting against each other.

I am annoyed with myself for feeling a wave of self-consciousness; I always do feel this way, at first, to have someone see me as I am, especially someone I used to be able to see, and maybe especially a former servant. Even though Honor as a child must have gotten used to my increasing loss of sight, I doubt she realized how close to blindness I was, and I'm stupidly embarrassed now in front of her. She has grown quite a bit taller, I'm guessing. Well, she could only have been eleven, that winter she left us, when Edgar was here. Her head surely just came up to my chin then, like Odile's now.

"How good of you to come," I say, unsure suddenly how I should address her.

"You're welcome, Madame."

Her voice is more womanly—naturally it would be. A trace of her childhood lilt still remains, though, I think.

"*Eh bien*, I am—well, you can see!" I gesture to all the invisible piles and boxes around me.

"*Oui*, Madame. How would you like me to start?" Her French is careful; she's been speaking English for many years, I can tell. I switch to English.

"Where are you living now, Mademoiselle Benoit?"

Honor is quiet for a moment, and then she says, "I live in Washington, Madame."

She is awkward to talk to, as I should have known she would be. I'm starting to regret Didi's hiring her today, much as I need her help.

"And are you—," *married,* I want to ask, but something prevents me. *It's none of your business,* I imagine her thinking.

"You were asking me—?" Something gentle has come into the prickliness of her voice, softening the edges. She pities me, maybe. I am well used to that, alas.

"Oh, it's nothing," I say. "Could you—? Maybe I should just stick all these things of Josie's in a chest, but first I at least want to know what in heaven's name is here. If I can go through these boxes today, then I'll be more ready to put this house in order. I doubt you have more than today free?"

I hear Honor picking up some papers and other objects. She doesn't answer my question about her schedule. Instead, she says, with a mixture of formality and warmth, "I am sorry for your recent losses."

I sense that she's been rehearsing this line in preparation for seeing me. So many people have said this, in precisely these words, I thought perhaps I'd become inured to the way such an expression of sympathy causes my disappeared children, out of the clear blue sky, to make a clamor in my heart. Jeanne and baby Henri first, Josie and Pierre to follow. I am not sure why this pinching and squeezing, as of a dozen little hands, does not take all the wind out of me and leave me limp entirely. I sit down on the nearest chair and make myself turn my face toward this young woman.

"Aunt Lily said it was the scarlet fever, that took Mademoiselle Joséphine?" she asks softly.

"Yes, and her brother Pierre. Do you remember him?"

"Yes, Madame, I do."

Hot, hot, Josie's forehead was, and soon after, Pierre's. Their throats so swollen, they couldn't talk. How quickly a life can flare up, like that, and then burn out. Eighteen years old, Josie. Pierre, eleven. And here Honor is, still alive, by the grace of all that is sacred.

"And you, Mademoiselle. I hear you lost family too, that way."

Honor murmurs something I cannot hear. *Oui*, Madame, I think it is. For one fragile moment, she and I seem to float in the same gulf of misery—different boats, but the same gulf.

"Have you been well yourself?"

"*Oui*, Madame. I've been well."

"And your mother?"

"Yes, Madame."

This is more than I could ever have thought to say to Honor when she was a child. Our relationship, I realize, is changing even as we talk, minute to minute. I'm unsure what it will be. She is utterly independent of me, and yet she is here, at Didi's hiring, and although I doubt Didi will pay her all that much, still, she is no longer a servant. She is from our nation's capital now, and by all I can tell, she's doing very well in her life, yet she's agreed to come to my new house on Esplanade for this job today. I wonder why. Somehow I doubt it's simply because she needs the money. Could she have another reason? The past is gone, and yet is it not here with us?

"How about you look through these clothes of Josie's, and see if you think any could be saved for Odile? I could have some altered when she's older."

Will Odile remember this poised young woman? As a small child, Odile used to be so attached, she'd cry when Honor went home for the day to her house a few blocks away, in Tremé. And after Honor left for good, Odile asked for her each morning, well into the spring.

As Honor goes through each box, she names the items and writes them down for me, in categories of to-be-kept, to-be-given-away, to-be-put-in-the-rag-bag or the trash: a green jacket, with pockets; a silk shawl, the color of cream; a penny whistle; a doll with a porcelain head and real hair the color of—here she hesitates, as if it's important to her to find the right word—of amber. And then there are the miscellaneous items significant to Josie and to no other person on earth. With these, Honor seems to grow embarrassed, as if I will fault her for the sorry contents Josie tucked away in a drawer or her doll house some long ago day: a tiny box of baby teeth, another of sea glass, another of newspaper clippings and advertisements for skin cream and bath salts.

Amid this catalogue of Josie's items, it comes back to me, how Honor helped me that winter of Edgar's visit. A girl as helpful as someone much older. She had a habit of humming slightly, just under her breath, old songs her mother or aunts must have sung to her. Sometimes I'd realize she was humming a song by Mendelssohn or Mozart I'd been singing, to the accompaniment of our neighbor America Olivier on the piano. I got so used to the child Honor's gentle music, I scarcely noticed, and yet it was a companion to my thoughts.

She tells me in bits and pieces, warming to me just enough to tell the top layer. She teaches drawing and painting now. I gather that she is a painter herself.

"Portraits, mostly," she says.

"Ah! That is a wonderful thing, Mademoiselle." I can't resist adding, "My cousin painted you, I think. Monsieur Degas. Do you remember?"

At first, I think Honor hasn't heard my question. I hear Gaston calling to Odile outside, a carriage ticking past.

Just as I am about to change the subject, she says in a low voice, "Yes, Madame. I do."

A silhouette, Mouche said. An ink spot. Possibly Honor detested the experience of modeling for Edgar, if that was all he could come up with for her face in the painting of the children on the doorstep. Everyone said what a lovely girl Honor was, as poised as a dancer.

Why she left our household I have no idea. I haven't seen her since the day or so following Jeanne's birth. The stories my family told me, later, seemed sketchy and garbled. I couldn't make head or tail out of them. Finally Lily told me, Honor's mother had decided to send her somewhere—I thought she said Charleston—to stay with a relative for a while.

My companion places a box of something in my hands.

"Mademoiselle Joséphine's china animals," she says.

Opening the tin box, I touch smooth porcelain. I know each one instantly: the cat with two pointed ears, the horse, the calf. And here are the two springer spaniels, one sitting, one standing, given to Josie by Edgar, shipped from Paris when she was about three or four years old. A gift from my mother, may she rest in peace: the rabbit with her three tiny babies, each one in a different position—crouching, sitting up, sleeping.

"Odile will love these," I say.

As we go through Josie's things, I find myself thinking, in spite of myself, about our neighbor Madame Olivier. I was excited that this accomplished woman could offer Josie piano lessons, and help to develop her voice. By the time Edgar and René arrived in those balmy days of late October, America Olivier had become a cherished part of our household. On Tuesday afternoons she came over to teach piano to Josie at 3:00 and then to Mouche's daughter Carrie at 3:30. On Wednesdays she came to our weekly at-home for friends and neighbors. On Thursdays she came in the morning for an hour to accompany me on the songs I'd chosen to sing at our Easter concert. On Sundays she and her husband Léonce would walk through the back gate and the wilder half of our garden, and up through the raised beds, to have Champagne and cake with us, and an impromptu recital.

How did America look to my sisters that winter? How did she look to René, and to Edgar? She must have appeared dazzling. I could feel the warmth of her arm as she slipped it through mine, and the gentleness of her hand as she touched my face after our kisses of greeting or farewell. Astonishing to think, she was only about twenty years old then, much younger than I was. Both she and I were pregnant that winter. Her baby was due in the spring—her second child—and mine in the days before Christmas—my fourth. Both of us were still nursing our small daughters. Whenever she walked into a room, I imagined she had some kind of golden cloud that hung about her as she accepted a glass of wine or a slice of apricot tart, sat at a piano, picked up a crying child.

For the first few times she came over, when Edgar was with us, he got oddly quiet, which seemed to me a sure sign of her beauty. Edgar clearly had a vivid life in Paris, and most likely he had come across many women—I had no illusions about the kinds of activities bachelors might enjoy—yet this young Madame Olivier, our neighbor, caused him to hush. In a way it was comical, but I also felt jealous. When I asked René to describe her, he claimed to find her ordinary looking, but Mouche said otherwise. It wasn't just her looks, though. It was her youth and humor. She was quick to laugh. She was intelligent, as I well knew. She also loved a party. There was something girlish about her, as if life hadn't yet started to wear on her. This was what I liked about her, in fact, in spite of my jealousy. She could make a quiet Sunday shimmer.

When Honor speaks, I jump.

"Pardon me, Madame," she says. "I was just asking about this sketchbook." She says this gently and yet with a certain intensity in her voice.

"Yes?" I say. I can feel my face growing hot. I had forgotten that Edgar's sketchbook must have been left visible on some surface or other in this parlor.

"Is this the sketchbook of Monsieur Degas? The painter? Your guest?"

I am startled by her boldness. It's as if she's holding Edgar's soul—his heart—his inner thoughts from a winter that somehow rises up now into this room, in this new winter. Water under the bridge? No, alas. This water is still flowing in swirls around me.

I resist the impulse to ask her to give the sketchbook to me. I resist the impulse to wrap it in the small satin dress I've been folding, and to place it quickly in a drawer, way at the back, until I can find a better hiding place.

Instead, I say, "Yes. It's a sketchbook of Monsieur Edgar Degas."

"May I—?"

I nod, aware of a new hope. Could Honor shed more light on this sketchbook than Odile or Didi could?

For many minutes, I can hear Honor studying the sketches that Josie may have cherished, reading the words that may have provoked Josie to hide them for herself.

•

I gave birth to Jeanne in the early hours of the morning of December 20th, 1872, just as dawn was breaking. As soon as she was born, I felt filled with light, to have come through that miserable labor, to have brought one more healthy baby into the world.

My water had broken after lunch on the day before, as I had walked out of the dining room, holding Odile by the hand. America had come to help for most of the afternoon and into the evening as well; she'd massaged my feet and my neck, as Mouche had popped in now and again with Baby Willie to kiss me on my forehead and cool my temples with a soft cotton towel dipped in rosewater. Didi, my stalwart, stayed throughout, as she had for my other children's births. Madame Bonaventure luckily was on hand too—the best midwife in New Orleans, a great comfort to me. René helped me by staying away, and keeping Edgar out of the house. They went to the Club with Papa, at least until it closed, so I could cry out in peace.

Lily brought food for America and Didi and a few other women who would come and go, chatting calmly in the midst of the storm of pain I was. Didi gave me sips of Papa's best brandy, a delicious, firy burning, and she let me squeeze her hand as fiercely as if I were a woman drowning.

I heard later that neither Edgar nor René had been able to sleep—little wonder!— and they wound up smoking cigarettes at the bottom of the garden, near the Oliviers' house, until Didi went outside just before dawn to give them both the good news. She said René wept when she told him.

How lovely that morning was, though. How lovely to hold baby Jeanne in my arms, cocooned in her cotton blanket, a tiny cap on her head. Her face, so soft, the softest, lightest silk, yet scrunched up too, like the quilted pouch that held my earrings. I felt sure I could see the daylight as it came in over the windowsill. I listened to Didi bustling about the room, then Lily coming up the stairs with a tray of coffee and cream, biscuits, an omelette. A little later, I could hear Honor calling to Pierre in the garden, and

Lily calling to all the children to come in for breakfast in the kitchen. Vasco da Gama barked as if to support Lily's request, and little Odile laughed. "Don't throw sticks!" Honor said, raising her voice. "Look at how pretty this lemon is, Odile! You can hold it."

As I drank Lily's strong coffee and buttered a biscuit, I chatted with Didi about the baby's upcoming christening at St. Rose of Lima. Edgar had been pleased to say yes to his new role as the baby's godfather. Didi made a list of friends and family to invite to the christening party at our house afterward.

Once the sun was so high that I could feel it on my face, and Didi had given the baby a change of clothes and placed her into the bassinet near me, I started to doze.

I could just hear Edgar talking to someone outside. "I'd like to have you in the picture," he said loudly. "Could you—please—sit right here. *Bien! C'est ça!*"

"Who is Edgar painting?" I asked Didi sleepily.

She walked over to the window and must have looked out. "Hmph," she said. "It looks as if he's painting Honor."

"Honor! But she has the children to watch!"

I started to pull my legs up and dangle them over the sides of the bed, trying to feel for my slippers. I could hear the baby snuffling in her bassinet like a sleeping kitten.

"No, you don't, Tell. You stay right there and rest up. I'll tell one of the maids to make sure the children are all right. Lily's there too."

•

I listen to Honor breathing next to me on the sofa. I

imagine that she's holding the sketchbook on her lap, maybe open to a certain page, or maybe closed. Gaston and Odile sound as if they're in the back yard again. I hope they're not bothering Hattie's spot for a kitchen garden. Odile is chastising Gaston for teasing the cat. "Let it have the food, Gaston!" she's saying. "You would not want to be teased, if you were hungry."

And I don't want to have this memory, but I do. It comes to me powerfully, like some large-winged angel, intent on its business, before I can fend it off.

It was on that morning, following Jeanne's birth, when I heard Josie shouting. She slipped into my room soon after, in tears, and thrust something at me. I was nursing Jeanne then—she'd latched on well, thank heavens. I was feeling the first pinpricks in response to her suck.

"Hush now," I said. "What is it? What can be the matter on such a beautiful morning, and with your new sister just born?"

Josie climbed up onto my high bed and pushed her face into my neck. She sobbed as if someone beloved had just been swept out to the Gulf in a hurricane.

She tried to collect herself, although her sobs were still coming like hiccups, as she pulled one of my hands from the baby's swaddling, and put a piece of paper into it—two pieces.

"What's this?"

"It's a sketch," she said. "It *was* a sketch. Cousin Edgar made it."

I felt the good thick paper, a ragged line along one side of each piece.

"What happened?"

It sounded as if Josie was rubbing her nose with her sleeve.

"Honor tore it."

"Honor tore it! How?" I couldn't picture that, not at all. Honor was a gentle child, a good servant. I never once knew her to even so much as pinch one of the children, or pull a strand of hair out of frustration. Yes, she was a bit of a dreamer, even her aunt Lily confessed as much. But she had nothing in her of willfulness that I had ever sensed; the most willful she'd ever gotten had been under Josie's urging.

"Joséphine, how did this happen?"

I waited, as the baby sucked more gently, and gradually seemed to have fallen asleep, letting my nipple pop out of her tiny mouth. I drew a light cotton blanket over my breast, and with one hand smoothed the damp hair off of Josie's warm face.

"She stole it," Josie said.

"Honor? Stole the sketch?" I wondered at that. "But why?"

"She said Monsieur Degas had tossed it into the trash."

"Why did he do that?"

"She said he always does that with sketches he doesn't like, except for the ones in his sketchbook. He leaves those in."

"So this was a sheet of paper that was separate?"

Josie was less agitated now, her breath coming more slowly.

"What's the sketch of?"

Josie was silent.

"Joséphine? I am asking you a question."

"It was of Honor," Josie said softly. "Her face."

I couldn't quite picture it. "So you're saying that Honor found a sketch of herself in cousin Edgar's trash, and she decided to keep it."

"She stole it."

I thought about this.

"If she wanted the sketch, Josie, then why would she tear it?"

"I don't know," Josie said uneasily, and I could tell she was fibbing.

•

"Honor," I say now, filled with this memory. "*Mademoiselle.*"

How do I ask what I wish to ask? I plunge ahead, because here, after all, is Edgar's sketchbook, and here is Honor, both of them in this house with me just for a day. If I am ever going to ask, the time is now.

"I have been wondering—forgive me, but—why did you leave that day?"

"Madame?" Honor sounds alert, startled.

"The day my daughter Jeanne was born? When Odile was one, and Joséphine was ten? When Monsieur Degas was our guest? You remember, don't you?"

"I—." Honor hesitates. "I am not sure."

If only I could see her face! Faces tell you so much. Didn't Didi say something else about Honor, as I lay in my bed after the birth, and she looked out the window? Didn't she say something about seeing René talking to the child, near the gate to the back garden?

The noises in the kitchen have gotten quieter, and I

can tell Hattie is listening to Honor and me.

"Come with me into the second parlor," I say, my heart like a hot, half-melted knot in my chest.

Honor lightly touches my elbow, to guide me. I'm grateful, and yet I say, "Thank you, but don't worry. I know where the furniture is now. It's just these boxes all mish mashed together on the floor."

I feel foolish, walking out of earshot of my servant, in order to question this young woman who used to be our servant. What seemed like calmness and airy space in this house now seems vastly lonely.

I sit on the sofa, and touch the spot next to me. Honor joins me on the sofa, although further away, I sense, than that spot. I can feel the air charged between us. Does Honor feel captured? Would she go off, if she felt she could?

"I didn't even say goodbye to you that day, Honor. I didn't know you were going. Whose idea was it?"

Honor seems to be absorbing my question, turning it around in her mind. I sense that a few answers come to her, before she hits on the one she says.

"It was—my mother's idea."

"Ah. Your mother's."

Honor's mother Eleanor came to the house once in while. She sewed hems and tears for me. Once, she made a dress for Josie, a muslin with a sash of robin's egg blue. She was a fine seamstress.

The Benoits' house, a few blocks away, was a small cottage, with a dozen steps leading up to a fanciful porch. From the years when I could still see, I remember sunflowers in the yard, along with a profusion of herbs in pots. The packed dirt was always swept clean. Honor's father had died when she was little. I had heard rumors that he had been brutally killed by the Union occupiers, during the War, but Mouche said it had been an illness. He had been a free colored man, of some distinction. After his death, his family fell into poverty. Instead of going to school, Honor became a servant, and her mother started sewing for hire. Lily had often brought Honor to our house, when she was little, so we had known the child many years.

"I thought your leaving had to do with something Joséphine told me about that morning."

Honor appears to be on the alert, as if I will say more.

"The sketch that got torn," I add. "Do you recall that business?" I rush to add, "It makes no difference now, absolutely no difference in the world. Joséphine told me the sketch had been thrown away by Monsieur Degas, so clearly he did not want it. I've just been wondering, because of this sketchbook Odile found today."

What I don't tell her is that around that time, Josie started to mope about the house. At first I thought it was the baby's birth that had made her so listless, but in fact she would let Jeanne hold onto her finger for minutes at a time, and she'd talk to her confidingly. What I sensed in Josie, more, was that she was missing someone, or grieving, and I couldn't help but think it might be Honor she missed. After all, in spite of the differences in privilege and color, she and Honor had been companions in the back garden when they were small.

"I do, Madame," Honor says. "I do remember a sketch." I think she will say more, but she doesn't.

"Josie told me it tore. Well, she said you tore it." I add, with my hand fending off any worry, "And I don't care about that now, it's all just one more glass of spilt milk, and there's no reason to cry over it, especially at this distance of time. But what I want to know is, is that why you left? Because you didn't have to, you know."

I am uncomfortably aware that I'm searching for some other answer too—to what question, I'm not sure. The only one I can think of is, why would René have been speaking to Honor? From what Didi had said that day, it sounded as if he'd kept Honor there by the gate for more than a minute. I couldn't remember a time when René had ever spoken directly to this child servant, or really had anything special to say to her. The servants in general were the responsibility of my sisters and myself. Sometimes he'd make a request of Augustus about the trees or flower beds, but that was different, and I'm pretty sure Didi often took it upon herself to alter René's orders, because as I heard her saying to Mouche one day, he knew about as much about gardens as a peahen.

Honor says, "No. No, I did not go because of a sketch."

"Then—?"

"It—. It was something I—." Honor pauses, and then changes tack. "My mother wished only to let me continue my education, and she thought Washington was the best place for that. One of my aunts lived there. My mother thought it would be better for me."

I am grateful to Honor for saying this much. I doubt she's told me the bigger truth. I feel that she and I are standing on a flooding plain, water lapping around our ankles, our feet sinking into mud. Urged on by some yearning I can't claim to understand, I turn to her.

"Well, Honor, in any case—could you kindly do me a

favor? Could you—describe this sketchbook to me, page by page? I know it's a great deal to ask of you. I will tell Mademoiselle Musson, my sister, that you've helped me with the boxes, and she will of course pay you for your labors. It makes no difference to her, what work you're doing. She doesn't have to know, to tell you the truth."

I wait for a long moment, and I expect Honor will diplomatically swerve around such a task. But she surprises me, and makes me flush with gratitude, as she says, *"D'accord,* Madame. I will do this."

I hear pained eagerness in her voice, and a great certainty comes to me, that whatever information she is holding back is something that still bothers her. I think of the way René wept at dawn, the morning of the baby's birth, with Edgar beside him. I think of the way Josie sobbed on my bed a few hours later. I think of America Olivier's fragrant hand on my face, and the parrot's cry in Honor's voice, *"Viens! Mais qu'est-ce que tu fais alors!?"*

How easily things can tear. Is that what Edgar wrote? It was Edgar who tried to do the tearing, though. He decided to make his own body something that could tear and bleed. Does his sketchbook describe what he did? Does it offer light? I yearn to look into it, in spite of my fear. It must bear some kind of witness to our life that winter, at least from Edgar's point of view.

"Let's begin," I say, and Honor begins. She must have had the sketchbook with her all this time, maybe right on her lap.

5

"Here is a sketch of your old dog," says Honor.

"With his tongue hanging out?"

I can tell she is smiling. "Yes."

I am filled with a sudden impulse to tell this young woman the truth about all kinds of things.

"You know, Vasco da Gama guarded our house and gardens like a four-legged angel."

I picture Honor smiling again. "I remember him," she says. "I was afraid of dogs before I met him. He was a good dog."

"I gather he was ugly, but I agree, he was good."

I tell Honor how Odile wandered out of the garden one day. I think it was in the spring after Edgar had left. She must have slipped out of the gate and started toddling along the street behind our house. Vasco da Gama barked and barked. He stayed with her until America Olivier saw the two of them, and brought Odile back.

"Ah," Honor says.

Honor starts to read, and my cousin Edgar comes right into the room.

•

New English words: yellow (jaune)
sky (le ciel)
tree (l'arbre)

face (le visage)

baby (l'enfant)

window (la fenêtre)

dog (le chien)

arms (les bras)

a child's face   luminous

•

"Does he have a sketch of a child there?" I ask. "Near that word luminous?"

"Yes."

"Which one, can you tell?"

"I think—I'm not sure, but I think—this one is of Mademoiselle Odile, when she was very little. One of just her face . . . one of Mademoiselle Carrie too, but you can only see a little of her face. A sleeping baby, maybe that's Master Willie, Madame Bell's."

•

Beauty (la beauté)
Light (la lumière)

Light blue (bleu clair)

how many colors for skin—rose, cream, macaroon, cinnamon, ebony, wheat

> *a mélange*
> *what is color, after all? How fiercely it is made to mean something   how impossible*

•

Honor is quiet for a moment, and then she says, "My aunt Lily is in one of the drawings on this page. She's hanging a sheet on the clothesline behind the kitchen. Also, I think this sketch is of me, holding a baby."

"You think it's of you? Are you not sure?"

"I don't recognize myself exactly."

A silhouette, an ink spot—is that what Mouche said about Honor in the painting? I wonder if this is the case in this sketch too. I can't ask Honor directly.

"Does he show your face?"

Honor hesitates. "He shows my face, but it's in such shadow, and I'm looking down and away. I'm on the step with the baby in my lap."

•

"This is a sketch of you, I think, Madame," Honor says.

•

E's muslin dress, a cloud of cotton, sprinkled with seeds or flowers
     myth

Work with blankness

the invisible blank walls of house   of memory?

•

A rush of something into my heart. "E" for Estelle? I wore just such a dress, when I sat on the *chaise longue* as Edgar painted me. He'd only just arrived, and I hadn't given birth to Jeanne yet. I made him promise not to show my belly, as big as a laundry basket by then. I didn't think to ask him not to show my blindness. I had always been told you couldn't tell, because I'd had my sight most of my life, and I assumed Edgar would show me to be normal. I should have known, remembering his first portrait of me, in the French garden. Possibly I thought he'd learned to flatter me.

"Is this part about blankness—this goes with a sketch of me, you said?"

"*Oui, je crois,* Madame. I think it's of you. It doesn't really look like you. *Peut-être.* You are sitting on a *chaise longue.* You are looking away, off to the distance."

"Am I pregnant?"

"I can't tell."

Mouche tsk tsk'ed over that small painting of me in my muslin. "It makes you look fat, when you were simply pregnant," she said. "Well, I told him I didn't want to be shown pregnant, Mouche!" "Very well, understood, yet he makes you look so—plain, so—vacant, as if your soul is absent. You're much more splendid than this, Tell!"

The invisible blank walls, E's dress, sprinkled with seeds, or flowers, myth. What myth did Edgar have in mind, I wonder? And were the walls blank to him or to me?

•

"Here is another one of you, Madame. You are standing in this sketch. You're holding a flower, putting it into a vase."

•

One tries to catch the real, but how can one be sure of it?

•

"Could you describe—how I look, in this flower one?"

"How you look?"

"Do I look—well, how would you describe it?"

Honor takes a deep breath. "You look—well, peaceful, I suppose."

"And what are the words, again, that Monsieur Degas wrote on this page?"

"*One tries to catch the real, but how can one be sure of it?*"

What did Edgar mean? I feel lightheaded. Strange, to have been such an object of Edgar's sight that winter. I had not felt that important to him, had I?

•

a dream's architecture
in English: "dream"

"wall"
"nothing"

•

"Then here are some things written in ink along the edge of the page," Honor says. "And a drawing of a hand, holding a paintbrush. Another hand. Eyes. Eyes, and the start of a nose; this looks like a drawing of Monsieur Degas' own face, but it's incomplete."

"What are the words?"

•

my eyes—pain holding on, a cormorant holding on to a prize fish

blankness at the center
without my sight, I am nothing.

•

I feel a wave of pity for Edgar, as I often did that winter. All this he poured into his sketchbook! Frightened, indeed, he must have been. To want so desperately to be a good painter, and to feel that his sight was slowly being stolen from him.

"Then, here," Honor is saying, "a woman is sitting in a chair, all wrapped up in a—it looks like a blanket, but perhaps it's a cloak."

"Who is it, can you tell?"

Honor appears to be thinking. "I cannot say. It's—

possibly your neighbor. It is hard to tell."

I sense by her voice that she is self-conscious now, and holding back. Of course her aunt Lily would have told her about what happened with America Olivier. And I feel stupidly betrayed by Edgar, to have drawn America in this sketchbook. Didi hadn't told me that, and neither had Odile.

"How would you describe Madame Olivier in this sketch, Honor?"

Honor seems to ponder this question, or how to make a diplomatic response.

"She looks as if she's waiting for something, or—. You can scarcely see her, she's so wrapped up in the brown material."

"Do you recognize the room in our old house, where she is? Is she sitting, or standing?"

"She's sitting in a chair. It looks like a plain wooden chair. I don't recognize the room. The sketch isn't that detailed, about the room. A few words are along the margin, near the center of the sketchbook, I mean along the central fold."

•

get these colors right
veils of yellow, green . . . light, rich, saturated
                    waiting

                              birth, a great rending
the bed's betrayal

•

"'The bed's betrayal?'"

Honor pauses for a moment, answering my question by her silence.

"And here's a bed, sketched lightly, just one part of it. And a sketch of a woman."

"Is she looking straight out at you?"

"No. She's looking at something you can't see. Oh, and here's another one, on the next page. She's sketched in, and with a high door frame around her."

"Could she be in the hallway outside my bedroom, Honor? Does that look possible?" I realize too late that I've called Honor by her first name. If she feels offense, she doesn't show it.

"It's hard to say, Madame. The space is blurry."

Yes, I think. Maybe that was it. I shouldn't forget how America held and stroked my feet, my arms, during my labor. Pregnant herself, maybe she rested in the hallway just outside my bedroom, waiting to be called in for more help. Could Edgar have sketched her then? He wasn't there, though, was he? He'd gone to René's office that day, to let him know my confinement had begun, and they'd gone out for dinner, and then to the Club. Of course, he could have posed her later.

I remember wondering if Edgar was drawn to her. I trusted that America could fend off all would-be lovers, including my awkward cousin, so elegant and so unsure of himself.

•

Art is like life, then. It can hold inside itself the secret of great pain.

•

"Could you say that again, Honor?" I ask.

As Honor reads this part again, Edgar's words bring him even more poignantly into this room. *The secret of great pain.* I picture him leaning on the doorjamb of this new parlor, or sitting on the chair near us. I picture him rubbing his eyes. The sunlight contained tiny arrows, he told me, that sliced through his irises. I could not see him then, and yet I believe I can see him now.

•

Think about this. Is there an art without pain?

•

"And the drawings near this observation, about art and pain?"

"Just a window, Madame. I think it's the view out Monsieur Degas' window, on the first floor, because I can see the lemon tree."

I remember now, it was sometimes Honor who brought Edgar's warm water to him, for bathing, in one of our porcelain bowls. A girl so reed-like, slender and sturdy. Like the whir of a wing in my chest, for a moment, it comes back to me, how I missed her once she was gone. I do not think I articulated this to myself. After all, she could be easily replaced. How could she have had the power to make us miss her? She had a brave soul, though—I felt this then, and I feel this now.

"Are there any people in this sketch, Mademoiselle?"

"You can see my uncle Augustus in the garden, off in a far corner. He's bending over, digging in a bed. Oh, and you can see a wooden hobbyhorse lying on the path."

•

must write to Tissot, Dihau, Papa, Thérèse, Marguerite
    eye specialist: M. Salomon, on rue Ursulines, near Royale

                                 tailor—M. J. P. Beauville,
                                      near the cotton office

my mother's family—odd, how scattered it is,
    across the color line
    Rillieux family, all across New Orleans

        rosy white children in ebony arms
        cinnamon arms

•

"Go on, Honor."

She has been quiet for half a minute, and although I am embarrassed by Edgar's mention of our family's colored relatives, I know this is nothing new to Honor. You can't grow up in New Orleans and not know everybody's business. It is not something to talk about, however. Edgar was a witness, perhaps, trying to interpret.

"Here—here's a drawing that could be of you, Madame."

"What am I doing in it?"

"Sitting in a chair. Sideways, though." Honor sounds almost apologetic, as if I will fault her for the sketch, and not Edgar.

•

keep the source of light uncertain

Shadows are our thoughts made visible.
get the eyes right

•

"Can you tell if I—. Do I look as if I have my sight?"

Something in Honor's manner changes. I picture her sitting up very straight and studying my anxious face.

"I would say, you do not look as if you are looking at anything. There is a vagueness to the eyes in this sketch. You are very much in shadow."

I remember posing that way, sideways in a chair. Edgar painted that one after the baby was born. Mouche and Didi hated it, and told Edgar so.

"I'm in a chair, you say?"

"Yes."

"Is there a table in front of me?"

"—I think so. It's hard to tell."

"With jewels on the table? A bracelet? Gloves? Earrings?"

Honor is quiet for a moment. "I don't see those things in this sketch. I see just the hint of a table and a big vase.

Ah," she adds. "On the next page, there are some words, by themselves."

•

(how blind I have been!)

(how could I not have seen what was right in front of me?)

(I think of my first days in New Orleans now as if from a great distance—when all seemed cheerful and good, the boundaries clear. I don't want to have sight, if it shows me terrible things.)

Orpheus—
how does one rescue one's beloved,
only to look at her and in that instant lose her again?
He is a criminal, in spite of the fact that he tried to save her.

•

So was I Eurydice to Edgar, then? *Sprinkled with seeds and flowers.* Caught by the king of the underworld, and taken into his dark realm? If blindness was that king, then yes, I did have to go live in that place of no sight. I live there still, in a sense. Yet I wish I could say to Edgar: this isn't my true habitation, not as I see it. I have not been as isolated or lonely as Eurydice was, thank heaven. My world is still all around me: the two children remaining to me; Didi; Papa; Hattie; my friends; my children's cousins; this house; this city.

And I have to wonder: did Edgar think he was my

Orpheus? What could that mean? What rescue did such a self-proclaimed Orpheus botch?

It was Edgar who needed rescue that winter, much more than I did. I'd had no hint of it—at least, no hint that I could understand. Yet he was the one to walk willingly into the underworld, to plead for it to close around him.

Honor has been describing more sketches, more words, but I am finding it hard to pay attention. I'm remembering how I found Edgar, that day before Epiphany, ten years ago to this day. Thank Mary the mother of God, and all the angels, that I did.

•

If I could pluck out my eyes
    so I could see nothing nothing   a blank
      shadows merely
    am I helpless to change [the thing]?
        It is frightening, this ++++
  So little remains, then
agony

•

I am moved, hearing Honor read these words. I am sure I should ask her to stop—this is too private by far—but, God forgive me, I am immersed now. Honor will be gone soon, this sketchbook just a memory for her. And I see now, perhaps Edgar did write about that day after all, not directly but more in the margins, as hints toward what he might have wanted to say outright. I'm glad Didi didn't come across this part. *Agony.* I couldn't bear her mockery of Edgar. She always felt he was overly dramatic. She couldn't have known what he chose to do.

"What are the sketches here, Honor?"

"Actually, on these two pages, facing each other, it's only words. Here's the second page."

•

winter and spring come at the same time here—flowers, weeds—softness of the air.

Without sight, could [someone] be happier?
To be blank, in a blank world
no color   no shape
No, it would be impossible
But still, knowledge is a terrible thing—God take such knowledge from me

All is bankrupt   one is helpless to xxxxxx

•

What in heaven's name is Edgar writing about? Could it be knowledge of Papa's bankruptcy, that came right after Epiphany? Poor Papa, to lose his position at the cotton office. Didi tried with all her might to rein in our expenses, after that, yet it was difficult. I'm not sure we would have come through that winter, if Uncle Auguste had not lent us the large sum in December.

"I wish I could help your family," Edgar said one day.

He was painting me as I held a sheet of music, with one arm out, pretending to sing. "It is terrible to feel powerless to help."

•

Honor says, "Then, when you turn the page, you see that one page has been left blank. And on the right sheet, there is small handwriting. It goes sideways along the inner fold. I see just a few words here."

•

(January.)

(She has saved me.)

•

"Honor, I am sorry. Could you read that again?"
"*January. She has saved me.*"
"Is there more?"
Honor's voice is hushed as she reads.

•

*(I am saved,
but for what?)*

•

Salt stings my eyes, and I do have to cry now. I take the

handkerchief from my pocket, and cover my face.

I had had no idea how bad it had gotten for Edgar. In the midst of our busy family life, babies, dogs, meals to be cooked, laundry to be done, children to bathe, Christmas, the pulling of weeds, the Champagne and plum tarts, the breakfasts, the messy house, the bankruptcy, the mounds of bills, the organizing of the servants, the purchases of shoes, the scrubbing of floors—in the midst of all this, what had Edgar experienced? How did he see us? What did he see? Did he look at his gloomy face in the mirror?—not straight on, because he couldn't see straight ahead, but only in the periphery? Did he think of writing a farewell letter to us, instead of leaving us with great blank whiteness, a great nothing, a transparency, where he himself had been?

Such a selfish thing, to try to take your life, isn't it? If you succeed, you rip the whole fabric around you; you touch each life and change it forever. An event like that, if it's not stopped, tears others' lives in two, like so many cotton blouses.

Yet still, I felt sorry for him. My heart broke for him. I thought it could only have been a powerful despair that led him to such an act.

•

"There is a jump of a couple of pages here," Honor is saying. "Monsieur Degas starts with a new pen. I see one sketch of Mademoiselle Joséphine, reading, with her legs curled up beneath her. And here's one of Mademoiselle Joséphine lying on a couch, wrapped up in a sheet or something of that nature. Here is one of your dog; he is asleep, stretched out, on a garden path. Then, a man by a—it looks like a table filled with cotton. A man reading a newspaper—I think this is of Monsieur René De Gas. Someone sitting on a stool looking at papers. A wastebasket filled with paper."

I remember Josie posing for Edgar again, during the podiatrist's visit and afterward. I can just imagine René reading the newspaper, as he did each morning at breakfast.

•

how light cotton is   how risky
  What's left, but making cotton out of my art, making my
    art into cotton?
  What will sell? That is the only question I can care about now.
                              I am only for selling now.
              All else is impossible.
  I refuse to drown.

•

"Here are more sketches of men in suit coats." She adds, "White men."

"Does it look like a cotton office?"

"I am not sure. Yes, it could be that."

I'm remembering how Edgar drove himself hard, in February of that winter, to do at least one larger painting that he could gain good money for. He threw himself into it as if it were the only thing that could save the entire world from ruin. René and Mouche's husband William were more absorbed in their silly costumes for the Crewe, and there was Edgar, slaving away at his painting, that we felt few people would ever see, or pay for.

•

Looking back over this winter, I see—could it be, that this is the consolation of art, could it be she is right, at least, it's the only consolation I can think of now, here at the edge of the world:
> *"You can paint what you see. You can paint the central blankness, the blurriness of the margins."*

•

I am certain by the sound of her voice that Honor knows I was the one who spoke those words to Edgar. The sun shines on my neck, my back. It is strange, but for a moment I feel an upsurge of happiness.

•

> *"At least you have that," ___ said, "and you can make something great of that, something extraordinary."*

What else? Write it down, before it vanishes:
> *"Do lines fade for you now? Then let go of the lines; think of them only as the ideas of lines, and they will hold, invisible.*
>> *Can you not see your neighbor's face? Then let the face be seen in passing, glimpsed in movement.*

Accept the blur that is life."

How do I tell her, it is not my sight only I am mourning?
It is not only my uncle's bankruptcy and infinite debt,
or my paintings not selling.
How do I tell her, it is something more that touches on her life profoundly.
How does she not know this?

•

I am listening very carefully now, but I am in over my head. It is immensely frustrating, to have these words flow past me, invisible. I can't catch hold of them.

"Are there sketches in this part, Honor?"

"A few."

"Of—?"

Honor's voice sounds a little thicker. "Well, here are one or two sketches of me, Madame."

"You? Ah! Describe them."

"*Eh bien,* Madame," says Honor, humming for half a second, distractedly, "one is of my face, looking straight out. And one is of me walking through the back gate, coming into your back yard from the neighbors' house."

"How do you know you're walking from their house? Did you pose for that sketch?"

"I can't recall that I did." Honor seems to be thinking. "No, I'm sure I didn't."

"You say he sketched you coming through the back gate?"

"Yes."

"Do you think he sketched that from memory?"

"I—I don't know, Madame."

Describe all of this more carefully, Honor, I want to say. I could weep from the desire to see the sketchbook. If I could study each image Edgar drew, maybe that winter could be clarified, and all that happened in it.

"Is there more?" I ask.

"A little. Here is one of your neighbor singing, holding sheet music. Her hair is up in a bun. She's in a morning gown; it looks like patterned muslin, with a fine, loose jacket." Honor adds, "Well, she's not exactly singing. She's holding up one arm, as if to protect herself from a blow."

I hear a page turning. "And here's another woman, in another pose. I don't think it's you, Madame. It could be, though. She's holding her music to her chest, and looking as if she is stepping forward. She looks as if she is pleading with the other woman about something. She is holding her hand out in a plea."

I remember holding my arm out with the palm up, as I held the music with my other hand, close to my chest. I felt embarrassed, holding my mouth open, so Edgar let me just stand there, mostly, as if I were about to sing. Sometimes I sang a line or two for him.

•

safran (saffron)

blanche (white)

les murs (walls)
un piano demi-queue (baby grand piano)

crépuscule (dusk)

rouge (red)

•

"And here is a sketch of a man at the piano. He's like a dark shadow, very fuzzy. I am sure he's a white man, though. The painter—your guest—put words here for colors— saffron for the walls, white for a couch. Here's a picture of the *chaise longue*, covered by a white coverlet, and with *rouge* written on a—shawl—or some kind of light blanket, lying across the top of the chair."

"I see."

I recognize the images that would go into the painting Mouche and Didi described to me, of a song rehearsal.

"What is Edgar thinking, with that blotchy red thing on the *chaise longue*?" Mouche said to Didi one morning after breakfast, once Edgar had headed off to write letters at René's office.

Didi sighed. "I don't know. It looks like blood."

Mouche laughed. "Does he think someone has committed a murder in our parlor?"

"I can't tell you, Mouche. Edgar likes drama. It's more like a scene in an operetta than a friendly portrait of Tell and America singing."

"It looks as if Edgar changed his mind about some things, and then didn't follow through. I mean, did you notice he changed the position of Tell's hand? She had it palm upward, and then he changed it to this gesture of 'Stop!' But you can still see the ghost of the other hand."

"Very strange," Didi said. "The same with the *chaise*— it looks as if he started to cover half of it over, to erase it."

"I thought that was a brown coverlet," Mouche said, laughing again.

"Who can tell? The floor looks brown too. More like mud," said Didi. "As if one could sink into it."

"Well, our house looks uglier than it is, that's all I can say," said Mouche. "And, Tell, I've never heard a duet with you and America that sounded the way Edgar makes this one look!"

"And what about René?" added Didi. "He looks very shady indeed, sitting like that at the piano. He doesn't even know how to play the piano!"

"Is that René?" said Mouche, really laughing now. "I couldn't tell. I thought it was Augustus."

"Well," Didi said—and I could just picture her shrugging and shaking her head— "Who knows? Maybe Edgar will fix it. And maybe someone will buy it. There is no accounting for taste."

•

Hearing Honor describe these sketches now, I feel stung by a swarm of bees. By Edgar? Yes. Yet, more, by this idea of two women in some grand operatic conflict. Mouche was right, that America and I sang our duets without theatricality. We weren't concert singers, or opera divas. We were just neighbors who, as I thought, tried our best to keep our voices in tune, and grow in our repertoire.

I confess, though, it's more than this. I can't help feeling beset, for the thousandth time, by the memory of America Olivier in our house, day after day, for years and years, singing, playing the piano, drinking wine, helping with my children, laughing in conversation.

And I am beset too by the memory of a day in April, five years after that spring of Edgar's visit, when René erased himself out of our life together. By then, it was too late to plead about anything.

"Shall I go on?" Honor asks.

I nod, unable to speak.

She reads the words Odile found first.

•

the poem she taught me—this line is best:
"Love is not love which alters when it alteration finds"

*L*ove   not love

How easily things can tear

•

I have the sensation of trying to listen to what Edgar wrote here, even as I do battle with his words. I sense a glimpse of some understanding that might come. I want it to come, even as I hope with all my heart it does not come, not today, not ever.

I can't remember what more Mouche or Didi said about that painting of the song rehearsal, if anything. I can't ask Honor now, either, because she left weeks before Edgar painted it, and in any case, what would a child have noticed or remembered? It's with Edgar in Paris now, most likely, maybe growing dusty in some storage area, its face to the wall. Or maybe he's sold it, or painted over it. I doubt that he has hung it anywhere visible to the public.

I do remember that when I first posed for that painting, Edgar didn't tell me America and René would be in the painting too. He didn't tell me he envisioned a scene of conflict between these two women. I would have been much less happy to pose, if he had. I'd simply thought he liked my singing, and wanted to honor it. America was a good friend then. I would have been insulted for her sake too, that spring, if I'd known.

•

"Accept the flaw, and make it the gift."

["That's in quotation marks," Honor says.]

> *Can one learn to do that, though? It depends what the flaw is.*
> *Can one fold such agony into one's life, make it hold?*
> *Can it be carried back across the impersonal Atlantic?*
> *You can stare and stare at a bed of cotton, and discover no truth in it*
>
> *Despair*

Havana—
  to home—and what then? The rest of one's life
  love is here

It is terrible to see

alters

•

"And then there is one last section," says Honor. "It comes on its own, without drawings. Actually, it is on a loose leaf, placed here."

"Well, go on, then," I say, for it must be best to let it all come now, at once.

Honor reads a description of the city of New Orleans. Edgar appears to have written this on the eve of his departure. I almost can't listen, caught and struck as I am by some of the images: the city as a huge sleeping cat, washed and clean, or foul; something about Lake Pontchartrain's beauty. Something "glittering," something "humming." Lemon trees and orange trees. People of all colors. It moves me, in the wake of Edgar's despair, to discover in his own words how much he cherished about this city I love so much, in spite of all. What might have happened if he could have stayed, for a summer, another winter? Could he have felt healed? Could he have found comfort? Maybe even love?

I try to listen. This is my one, my first and last, chance to hear Edgar's words. It is as if a boat is leaving Mobile today for Havana, and all his words and drawings are on it. Already they become simply fragments in my memory and imagination. I fear that one day I will remember only the sensation of these hours with Honor, the emotions I have as she tells me of me this sketchbook, filtered through her own sensibility.

"*Most of all,*" Honor reads, her voice clear and yet distant somehow, as if she now has only one foot here, one foot in another world, "*I shall dream of faces open, clear as light, all colors, shining cream and rose, bronze, ebony, cinnamon . . .*"

Honor pauses. How does she think of this catalogue of colors? Is she remembering the sketches Edgar made of her, which may have looked so much more beautiful and precise and true than the ink spot he made of her in his painting?

"Yes," I say. "Is there more?"

"*Cinnamon . . . ,*" Honor reads, and pushes on, slowly, each phrase opening up Edgar's soul, window by window. It is about women holding babies, and two women singing. It's about a child servant. A woman whose sight is a blank.

"*. . . Such beauty—I could not have known there would be such beauty—and may I hold all of this in my heart, and in my inner eye; may I continue to open my eyes; and may her light always shine inside me, so.*"

6

Edgar's words float in the air around us.

"Have you come to the last word?" I ask.

Before Honor responds, I feel I must have dreamed her presence here beside me, on this sofa. I must have dreamed all these words written here and there, tucked in beside invisible sketches, and this last burst of Edgar's emotion—this prayer, wish, benediction, whatever it is.

"Is this it, Honor?" For she is Honor now. I cannot keep the distance anymore. I don't know how she feels toward me—I doubt she feels as I do, because why should she? Yet I feel almost as close to Honor on this day as I felt to Josie on her last. This is surprising, but it is true, and I hold the truth close. She is my link to my daughter—perhaps that is it.

"Is this it, then?" I ask again.

"Yes. I think so."

I sense that Honor is still looking at the sketchbook, although I don't hear her turning pages.

What did Edgar mean? I am moved that he appears to have thought of me—could I be the one he is describing?—as filling the world around me with love? But then, earlier, did he write about love as "terrible to see?" And then that word "alters." What is terrible to see? Is it love that is terrible, then? Or is it a terrible thing to see what should be hidden? Did he mean that love alters, and that this is what is terrible?

And what love was Edgar talking about? If he was talking about himself, I cannot be sure whom he loved with such sorrow and such despair. If he was talking about René's love altering—well, how in heaven's name had Edgar been so prescient? It's as if he could see into the future, to the day when his brother woke before dawn one soft April morning, five years ago, and walked quietly out of our house to meet America Olivier and her children at the train station, without so much as a kiss or a goodbye to any of us, still asleep in our beds.

I resist the urge to ask Honor to read the whole sketchbook again, this time describing each image with the utmost clarity, and giving me time to hear each word so fully that I will have more chance to remember it. The day is speeding ahead, however. And in any case, I am beset by a tumult of muddy grief.

What is to be done? All this happened a long time ago, and more has happened since. I think of Odile and Gaston, and wish them—will them—happiness. I am fierce in my determination to protect them from my own sorrows.

I sit up straight, breathe for a moment, and then say to Honor, "Well! Thank you for describing this sketchbook so carefully. I imagine you will be eager to move on from this task."

I am sure I don't fool her, though, not for a minute. She and I are in this together now, surely, the sketchbook open on the seat between us. And here is Edgar too. He is still here, in this new house. He is like a ghost, come back to tell me something I am trying with all my soul not to hear.

I set Honor the task of sorting some baby clothes

with me, yet I sense her heart is elsewhere, and so is mine. Maybe I should let her go home, and Didi will just help me tomorrow, once I am more myself. I can't tell Honor to go, though. I am more grateful for her presence than I can say. It is selfish of me, I'm sure, but she is the only one in the world now, besides Edgar, who knows each page of this sketchbook.

As I absentmindedly fold baby blankets, I can't help remembering those days around Christmas, when I thought all was well with Edgar. I can't forgive myself, even now, for my unawareness of Edgar's emotions. I remind myself that I was still recovering from Jeanne's birth, and it was hard to get sufficient rest. I felt that the demands of all my children, the baby preeminently, were often too much for me. René seemed in a distant mood, which upset me. I couldn't understand why he didn't seem happier with the birth of our third child together. I thought maybe it was because he had to wait until I had healed, before he could come to our bed with desire again. Patience was not one of his best virtues.

Yet, in spite of these worries, Christmas Eve was lively, with a big feast Lily and the other servants had concocted: oyster soup, bouillabaisse, saffron rolls, two kinds of sherbet, Gulf shrimp in a pepper sauce. Mouche brought a pillow for me, and set me up like a queen at the table. The Champagne—Edgar's gift—was delicious, and soon I was laughing and joining in the merriment. Before midnight Mass, the children opened presents, and I worried as always about the money René must have spent, yet I was happy too, at least I remember myself as happy. A new coat for Josie, and a yellow muslin dress; tops and little metal toy cars for Pierre; a tiny doll in a silk dress for Odile; a little stuffed hedgehog for the baby, and a christening gown imported from Italy. A pearl necklace for me, with a bracelet and earrings to match, and also a pair of the softest yellow kid gloves, which went almost to my elbows.

Those lovely gifts were the same ones my sisters remarked on, when Edgar put them into a painting of me, a few weeks later in January—the grave one, where I sat in the chair sideways, hemmed in by the shadowy table, my eyes blind, my hand a claw. On the table, the earrings, the bracelet, the gloves, as if I had shed them, or as if they had been offered to me. A transaction, in any case, Mouche said drily.

My sisters tried, with more or less success, to show diplomacy. They often thought Edgar presented our household as too dark, too filled with shadows or struggle, concocted out of the murky interior of Edgar's imagination, and this particular painting tipped over into the unforgiveable. "It's like a message from the Underworld," Mouche said.

I wondered, though, whether what Edgar came up with in a painting like that was simply the product of his anguished imagination. I felt like someone in a story, who's in a room, listening to the knocks of a stranger on the other side of a wall, and trying to make sense of them. I listened carefully to my sisters' descriptions of his paintings, yearning to understand what Edgar had created. Yearning, and yet disturbed too. Perhaps I didn't truly want to understand, after all. I doubt now that they wanted to understand either. Or maybe they understood more than they let on.

That Christmas Eve, however, I was happy. I am sure of it. I didn't know yet about Papa's business floundering and going under. It would be in a few days when that truth would come out. I didn't know either about René's cotton business barely holding its head above water. Business was all right, Edgar was fine, as far as I knew, and the baby was healthy. My family lifted our glasses and toasted each other, just as we always did. Edgar might have been a bit quiet, but I tried to ignore him.

At our Christmas Day gathering the following afternoon, I sang with America. The baby had slept a good five hours at a stretch, so I was starting to feel a touch more like myself again. The household felt lazy and luxurious; I imagined wrapping paper and ribbons still on chairs and under sofas, as a great indolence swept over us all. Lily had come in the morning for an hour or two, to make us our Christmas breakfast, and it was Didi who made the coffee that afternoon and set out the cognac and the trays of little apple tarts.

The duet I sang with America was by Franz Schubert, "*Wenn ich in deine Augen sehe.*" Edgar translated the German lyrics for us. Something about *when I look into your eyes, my grief* and something *vanish.* Then something like, *when you kiss me, I am healthy once more.* The last two lines come to me out of the blue.

Doch wenn du sprichst: "Ich liebe dich!"
So muss ich weinen bitterlich

Yet when you say "I love you," I must cry bitterly. Was that the translation? Sad, for a love song.

America's and my voices melded well together; the resonance could be felt to fill the front parlor, and even the children seemed to listen.

In the mishmash of emotion that winter, in any case, in the bustle and worry of birth and gifts and cakes and songs, I could barely think about Edgar. If I was honest with myself for a moment, I felt him increasingly to be like a wounded cloud, hovering in the corners of rooms, looming in hallways. When had he become that way? I couldn't say. All I could think was that, before baby Jeanne was born—his godchild—he had been a wonderful companion. He had sketched and painted for weeks; he'd created portraits that sounded at least interesting, if not beautiful; he'd enjoyed the children; he'd opened up to me about his hopes as a painter. It was a competitive field, he had seemed to be saying, and he was glad to be across the ocean for a while from the Salon with its favoritism and idiocy, and from the gallery where a dance picture he'd had great hopes for couldn't sell. He sounded bothered by the art market, and worried about his eyes, but nothing had seemed tremendously out of the ordinary. I felt sorry for him, being in a profession where the income was so uncertain, and the chance of selling your art so risky. Cotton at that time seemed more substantial to me, although I should have known better.

From day to day, then, Edgar had appeared to be fine, by and large. Yes, he had to protect his eyes, and his stomach had been weak. Yet he'd done some nice paintings, and he and René had been getting along well, I thought. Perhaps a little prickliness had grown up between them, but they were brothers, after all, with eleven years' difference in age, and of course Edgar was in the disorienting position of being a guest in a city unfamiliar to him. I remember wondering if he might be homesick.

•

I was the one who found him.

The weather had grown dismal, after all the sunshine of Christmas. Edgar had come down with yet another bout of dysentery, and had started to stay most of the day in his room on the first floor—Papa's library. I had been preoccupied with the baby that morning, and with Josie too, who seemed at loose ends, by turns bored and tearful. I had quarreled with René about Josie's schooling. I wanted her to stay with the nuns in New Orleans, and he thought she should go off to a Catholic boarding school in Alabama. Of course, as it turned out, she did, but that winter I held my ground, in spite of René's pressure.

Also, because Honor had left us on the day of Jeanne's birth, Mouche and I were more on our own with our children, until after the holidays, and Mouche had grown tired and irritable, what with caring for her own baby Willie, and Carrie, and mischievous little Sydney, who got into everything there was to get into, including the compost pile of weeds to the side of the back yard, where he discovered a dead rat one day, to his delight. Two of our maids had quit with little notice, and we only had Lily, Augustus and one house maid left.

Edgar was about to go home to France. All his clothes had been freshly laundered and ironed by Lily and the laundress who came to help her each Monday. He'd reserved a spot on the train heading up to Mobile, on January 7th, the day after Epiphany. From Mobile he would sail to Havana, and then to Le Havre. I couldn't imagine him travelling, though, when he couldn't even manage with the simplest food—milquetoast or chicken broth, the blandest white fish with no sauce.

Maybe if I'd had my sight, I would have known sooner how distressed Edgar had become. I don't know how I sensed that something was gravely wrong that morning of January 5th. I did sense this, though. The house maid reported that he hadn't let her come into his room to make his bed and bring him clean linens. I decided to bring him the linens myself, as an excuse to check on him.

When I knocked lightly on his door, I heard nothing. Ordinarily, I would have waited, but somehow I knew that I couldn't wait. I opened the door, and greeted him, as I walked into his room, yet he gave only the softest murmur, not of a name—more, just a sound. As I approached him I guessed he was at his dresser, near the wide porcelain bowl filled each morning with warm water for his shave and washing. I put my hand on his back, and through his cotton shirt, I could sense how he was trying to stand up, yet starting to slump.

I said, "*Mais qu'est-ce que tu fait, là!* What are you doing, Edgar? What is it?" as I moved my hand along his arms, the sleeves rolled up to his elbows. His left hand was under the water, limp. I had never touched him before in such a way.

"What have you done?" I said, panicked now.

"It's nothing, Tell. Go away," he said, or growled. If a person could growl, this is what he did, like Vasco da Gama once, when we had to pull the thorn out of his paw.

I felt the slick cut then, right on Edgar's wrist, and he

cried out; it felt like a small, bloody mouth. I moved my hand about the dresser, knocking off a glass or something, which crashed and broke on the floor. Holding onto him, I grabbed a linen cloth in the pile by his mirror, as I pulled his hand out of the water and wrapped the cloth quickly and tightly around his wrist. What on earth had caused him to do this? As I felt for his pillowcase, and shook the pillow out, as I tore the case into long strips and wrapped them too, I tried to remember some sign that must have slipped past me.

"Edgar, what in heaven's name is happening?" I said. My panic had turned to fury, and I couldn't think what I was saying. "I have my hands full with this household, and I've just given birth to my fourth child, and here you are, trying to kill yourself, right under my roof! I will thank you to pull yourself together, my friend, and to stop this nonsense right this minute."

I practically pushed him to lie down on his daybed, and then I thought to close the door to his room, and came back to bend over him. Outside the open window, I could hear Augustus raking a few yards away.

"Augustus!" I said. "Go tell Lily I need her, this instant, and then go to our doctor, M. Lejeune. M. Degas has taken ill. You will bring him here as quickly as possible. Go ask to borrow a carriage from the Duchamps family across the Avenue. If anyone asks you what you're doing, tell them this is my request."

Augustus said, "*Oui*, Madame," and I could hear Vasco da Gama barking as he followed Augustus across the street.

I helped Edgar off with his shirt, and then got Lily to bring a bowl of fresh warm water and some towels. I was grateful that René and Papa were out of the house, and Mouche was at America's house with most of the children.

"What is it, Maman?" Josie had knocked lightly, and she must have opened the door.

"It's nothing," I said, trying to make my voice sound light and normal. Lily was bustling about. I could hear shards of glass clinking. "Please close the door again, Josie, and leave us alone here. Cousin Edgar is feeling unwell. Lily is helping him, and a doctor will come."

"But what is wrong?"

"He just needs peace and quiet. All is well. Please go now. Go check to see if the baby is still sleeping upstairs."

I hoped fervently that Josie could not see around Lily and me. The basin must have been filled with bloodied water, and maybe the blood had gotten onto the floor, the bed, Edgar's shirt, Lily's apron. How would I know?

"*D'accord*, Maman. I am going," Josie said, and I could hear the door click shut.

I was determined that no one in the house, apart from Lily, should know what Edgar had done. I said to myself it had just been a mistake on his part, an idiotic error, and why should I draw attention to it? My sisters were exhausted enough by him. Best to pretend nothing had happened. Yet I felt I was in a dark quagmire, and couldn't find the edges of it.

It was later that night, once Lily had helped me clean up Edgar's room and soak his linens and shirts in cold water with bleach, and he was safely in bed, after taking some broth, that Josie confessed to me she felt she was the one who had made him so sick. I wasn't sure if she understood what Edgar had done, but she seemed to feel distressed, as if she sensed that his sickness went beyond a question of mere physical health.

"Why you, of all people, my darling? Why would you think you had contributed to his sickness? That's foolish." I had just put the baby into her bassinet for the night, and I felt like a miserable shell of myself. "You can come sleep in my bed," I added, in spite of knowing that this would irritate René.

As Josie came in under the duvet she said, "I thought it was because of the sketch."

"The what?"

I tried to think what she meant. I remembered, then, the two fragments in my hands as I had nursed little Jeanne the morning of her birth, over two weeks earlier.

"Joséphine, this has nothing to do with that sketch! I doubt that cousin Edgar gave that a second thought, if he even knew about it."

"But he hasn't looked at me since then," she said. "He hasn't smiled."

I stroked her hair. "I doubt that he's looked at any of us. He has had his own preoccupations." As I said this, I knew it was true, and more than true. How could I have been so unaware?

Her head moved in a little nod, and soon she was sleeping soundly, one arm draped around me, her head tucked into the spot she loved. I lay in bed next to her, worrying about Edgar, thinking back over the previous few weeks, listening for the sound of René coming home from the Club. All I could hear was someone walking quietly down the back garden, and then the back gate opening on its rusty hinges. I thought that must have been Papa, who had a neighbor a few blocks away he liked to visit, for cards. Possibly he had forgotten something at the neighbor's house, and had to retrace his steps. As I fell asleep, I tried to wash out the memory of Edgar's hand in the water. That hour in his room felt like a play I had witnessed, somehow outside of myself, not a real situation I'd actually been in. I had never felt so strongly the aching mystery of those nearest to me.

7

As Honor continues to do the sorting, I go quickly upstairs to my bedroom for a chance to collect myself. I can't collect myself, though. Instead, I feel bitterness and fury.

As I stand near the window, I imagine saying to Edgar's spirit, "You haven't proven anything yet. And in any case I do not have to listen to you. How have you showed your concern for our situation in these last difficult years? Even after my littlest one Henri died, I heard nothing from you. Even after your spoiled youngest brother left us. Even after Mouche died, that same year, after giving birth, and her baby died too. Even after your godchild Jeanne died, a month after Mouche. Even after Josie and Pierre died, within days of each other. Heartless, you are; you must be. I have no need of you, and no wish to hold you in my thoughts for one iota of an instant. I saved you, Edgar. I did save you—you acknowledged it—and this is how you repay me."

I have not known until this moment how wronged I feel by Edgar. It's as if a seawall has crumbled inside me, and I can't any longer prevent the water from flooding in. I can only try to swim in it. I do not know if I can find my way to shore.

I listen into the hush of midafternoon for some response from my cousin, across the ocean, but there is nothing.

•

That winter, Edgar was well enough for Epiphany, but he could not risk a trip across the ocean yet. The cut was smaller than it had felt, and I had caught him at the start of the act, thank God. The doctor had shown me how to clean and dress Edgar's wrist each day, and Edgar wore his longest shirt, with the silver cufflinks—as Josie told me, the ones shaped like seashells—to cover the dressing as well as he could.

I thought everyone in our household would notice, yet they didn't seem to. I only remember Didi asking him one day if he'd cut himself, and he said yes, he'd been trying to pick some lemons, and he'd scratched himself on the thorns.

"Well, ask me next time, Edgar," she said. "I have gloves you can wear, that cover your wrists and forearms."

On the Day of Epiphany, Lily made the King cakes, and the children dressed up as kings and shepherds and angels for a children's party Mouche held at our house with neighbors. America and Léonce Olivier came with their own Odile, dressed as a small angel in white, with a pink sash and a gold halo. Léonce had just come back from a trip to France, on business.

Edgar came into the dining room to watch as the children ate bowls of ice cream and drank glasses of punch. I put my arm through his for a few minutes, and I hoped that he was at least a little bit relieved, to be here with us still, listening to the sounds of children talking and laughing.

Once René started trying to lead the little guests in

charades, with the help of America, Edgar told me he'd just go have a siesta for half an hour or so, he was sorry he felt the need to rest. A couple of charades were mildly successful, but most of the children were too young to understand, and the party dissolved into jumping around and shouting, and a few tears, until America kindly offered to play music for them, and then they played Statue. They danced as she played, and once she stopped, they giggled as they froze in place. Vasco da Gama somehow got into the house then, and this game too exploded into shrieks of fear and delight. Didi handed each child a little King's cake trinket as a party favor, and by 3:00 the shepherds and kings had toddled off with their parents, and the house had started to resume its lesser chaos.

It was then that I sought Edgar out and talked with him alone for the first time since he'd cut his wrist. I sat in his room, on the stuffed ottoman. From across the hall, we could hear Josie playing a French Christmas carol.

"Why did you do it?" I asked him. "Can you be honest with me, Edgar?"

He moved in his chair, as restless as if I'd trapped him and bound him with silken cords.

"I can't say, Tell."

"Is it because of your eyes?"

He was quiet for a moment. I could almost hear him thinking, and yet I had no notion of what he thought.

"—Yes," he said. "My eyes."

"It's because your sight is being compromised?"

"Yes, Tell. My sight is being compromised."

I could hear something sarcastic in his tone. Well, of course, I thought—of course he would be angry, going blind as he was.

"It may go better for you, than for me."

"What?" he said quickly.

"Your sight. It may go more slowly. You may have your sight, even just your peripheral sight, much longer than I did, Edgar."

"Oh," he said, and I sensed him thinking about this, mulling on it. "I am sorry, you know. I'm sorry about your—sight. I haven't yet told you that."

"It's all right," I said, although that was a fib, and Edgar knew it. I'd been hurt that Edgar hadn't even raised the subject, after our first encounter at the train station.

"You are so beautiful, Tell."

I could feel my blush, from my chest into my face.

"I'm not giving you a compliment, just stating a fact. Your beauty is deep, you know. It's not only on the surface, although it's there too."

How ill at ease Edgar was. Instead of sounding loving and gentle, he sounded as if he were telling me something hard about myself. He was never very good at expressing the tender emotions. I sensed his kindness, though, disguised as it was, and I was grateful for it.

"But Edgar, you are changing the subject. This is not about me. It's about the thing you did—it was overwhelming. Have you been so unhappy here?"

He gave a short, angry laugh. "Unhappy? Me? What about you, Tell? Have you been happy?"

"But why do you turn the tables? I am not the one to cut my wrist with a razor in the middle of a fine winter day, my friend."

"I'm sorry, Tell," he said, and I did feel him to be so.

"I didn't think about the children. I didn't think about anything. I was just in some kind of pain, I can't describe it, and it's best left alone."

"Edgar, it will be all right, about your eyes. I promise you."

He laughed at that. It was more a noise than laughter, as if someone had squeezed his rib cage suddenly, and this was the sound forced out of his lungs. I felt frightened then all over again, because I thought maybe he had a touch of madness, so I started to talk, saying any foolish thing that came to mind, just anything, the way you'd croon to a small child who had been badly hurt, and I felt that he listened. This must have been what he remembered, to write down in his sketchbook, about doing the best one can, with the sight one still has.

8

Mid-afternoon, the piano arrives. By the sound of voices and shoes, three men have brought it, and are hauling it up the front steps like a sleeping elephant. I tell them to make sure they don't let it scrape the front door. Gaston is beside himself with delight and frenzy. Honor is unpacking the silver in the kitchen with Hattie.

"Don't get underfoot, Gaston!" I say. "Odile, please keep your eye on him."

Our piano has been in Odile's life since the weeks before Edgar's visit. I cherish it still, even though it added to our family debt. How can a piano be at fault for anything? It's just one more innocent bystander. Odile used to sit on my lap, banging on the ivory keys, or on the floor near Josie, when America would be playing the piano as accompaniment for a singing lesson. As soon as Odile could move her fingers along the keyboard, she asked for lessons, so at first I let her have five minutes at the end of each of Josie's lessons, and soon enough, before she could even reach the pedals, she had her own chance.

After her Papa walked out of her life with her piano teacher, however, Odile would not touch the instrument for months. Once Odile did come back to her music, each new song she played was something I celebrated inwardly, as if to say to America and René, you have not quashed our spirit. You cannot defeat us. We have our music still.

Once the piano's legs have been attached, and it has

been laboriously righted, I pay the men, and see them out the door. Odile sits down to play one of her favorite songs, a Mozart sonata she's been studying. She does well at the start, but stumbles as soon as it becomes a little harder.

"Slow down, Odile!"

"I'm not really playing, Maman. I'm just seeing if the piano is all right."

"It sounds as if it will need tuning."

"Maman, listen to this part."

Odile jumps to the section she knows best, and plays it with enthusiasm. I realize that she is hoping to impress the young woman who used to carry her up and down the garden, and pick lemons for her, and brush her hair. She might not remember Honor Benoit directly, yet something may linger in her memory. Odile plays more loudly than necessary, so that Honor can hear her in the kitchen.

•

The morning Jeanne was born, after Didi had told René of her birth and he'd wept in the garden, he came to our bedroom and kissed me on the forehead. He sat on the bed for a few minutes, and held my hand, bringing it to his mouth to kiss my palm, my wrist, as the midwife was giving the baby a sponge bath. Luckily I had not had to have any cuts made for the birth. I felt such love for my husband then. He kissed me again and said he hoped I would be able to rest now.

It was once the sun had come up, and I'd had my breakfast, with the baby all clean and sleeping in her bassinet, that Josie flew in to tell me about the torn sketch of Honor. I was pretty sure Josie had grabbed for it, and torn it. What had Josie said then, though? Something more, that I can barely recover. Something awful, like, "I hate your husband." Was that it? "I hate my stepfather." Was that it?

"Heavens," I told her, trying to quell my dismay, "if I could stand up right now, Joséphine Balfour, I would wash your mouth out with soap."

"I don't care, Maman," she said. "It would still be true."

And where was René by then, that morning? I try to remember. I try to hear his voice in my bedroom, singing to the baby or talking with me.

What I still can't understand is how René could have had two more children with me after Jeanne—how he could have helped me raise all five of our children, plus Josie, day in and day out, for years, only to throw it all over at the last minute, and fall at the feet of my friend. And I can't understand how America could have said yes! Yes, I will go with you! How is such a thing possible? She had been such a bright presence in our household, over those years. I had confided in her. She had confided in me! We were constantly going through the back gate with our children, or bringing comfort when one or the other of us or our children were sick. What could have happened in those weeks before René and America slipped away? To marry! Both of them were already married!

I could understand America falling in love with René, because I had fallen in love with him myself. But how could she have done this? And how could he? Was it because of my loss of sight? Is that what made my husband look at her? Or was she unutterably lovely?

Sometimes I think it must have been baby Henri's illness, our loss of him, that changed something vital in René. Henri was our last child—a great gift, as I felt then. Gaston had been a healthy baby and toddler, *grâce à Dieu*—and for a whole year our baby Henri too looked the picture of health, but he could not hold out against the fever burning up his small body. He was not quite walking yet. Maybe we should have taken the children out of the city, to the healthier countryside. And maybe something broke in René then, because it was the following April, five years ago, when he left. He abandoned all of his children, and me, while America walked out only on her bewildered spouse. She took her children with her, as if they were hers and René's. I gather that they live in Paris now, and have since had more children together. I wonder if Edgar has forgiven his brother. At first he assured our family that he could not forgive him, and I have a feeling he held out as long as he could, given his sense of honor, but René is clever and charming. Edgar always cared about him and tried to support him, in spite of René's recklessness. And I have not the slightest indication that my own family still holds a place in Edgar's heart. Why else has he been so silent? It hurts too much to think about it.

And this is what René missed, what he could not help me with, and for this I do not think I can forgive him: Mouche's death after childbirth, and the death of her baby; Jeanne, just a little girl, taken off with yellow fever soon after. And then, and then—just over a year ago—Josie at eighteen, Pierre at eleven, ravaged by the scarlet fever.

•

Honor has said she must be going home now, and both of us have stood up in the parlor.

"Honor, could I ask you one more question, just a little one?"

She waits, I think impatiently, her bracelets clinking.

"I'm just wondering—am I right, did you say that Monsieur Degas made a drawing of you coming into the garden from the back gate?"

"—Yes, Madame."

"Yet you didn't pose for him, by the gate?"

"I did not."

"Did he see you, though, coming through the back gate?"

Honor hesitates. "He may have. I often came that way."

"But on that morning—on that morning of the baby's birth—had you gone to—do you remember where had you been? Had you gone to our neighbors' house that day?"

I can sense I've touched on something.

"Which day?" she asks, wary.

"Your last day with us! It's something I'm just curious about. It doesn't matter, really."

I know she can see right through me, though.

"I had run off." She says this briskly, sharply, as if she has plunged into an ice cold lake.

I hold my breath for a moment, waiting to see if Honor will take the risk of saying more.

"I was just a child," she says, bitterness and indignation edging her voice. "I had been worried about the sketch. The one you mentioned. I thought I would be whipped over it tearing."

If I ask Honor more, she could walk out of the house in

an instant. She does not have to stay here, to be questioned by a Creole lady about something that happened when she was a child.

"Forgive me, Honor, but I am wondering: did you go home, then? Is that what happened?"

"Yes. No."

She sighs in frustration and anger. I'm sure she will tell me nothing more. The clock ticks, and yet I feel that time has come to a halt—or, time has bent back in a great circle to that earlier winter's day. Out of this pause, this large bending, Honor decides to say more. I am not sure why she does. It occurs to me that she too still thinks about that day. Somehow it still appears to be fresh for her.

"I started to go home, but then I thought better of it. I reached your neighbors' house, the ones behind you –."

"The Oliviers'," I say, my heart hot.

"Yes. And I—I don't know. As I passed by, I think I heard a child crying upstairs, and I looked over at their house."

"Yes."

"Well, there isn't anything to tell you about that. It's silly; it's nothing."

"Can you remember—did you see my husband, Monsieur De Gas?"

"I may have. I—I am not sure."

Where had he been? All morning, the morning of the baby's birth. *How easily things tear.*

"Did you talk with him?"

"I'm not sure. I think it's possible he spoke to me."

"Did you happen to see the painter, our guest, then too?"

"He was in your garden, I think, near the back fence, as I came back inside to fetch my things."

"To fetch your things?"

"Yes."

"You had already decided to go?"

"It—was not my decision."

"I thought you said it was your mother's decision?"

"It was my mother's decision to have me leave New Orleans, and to live for a while with my aunt."

"You lived for years there."

I sense that Honor is deciding how to respond.

"I liked it there." She says this simply, with a bright touch of defiance.

This is what I cannot ask Honor: *Did my husband offer you money? Did Josie see him do this?* I don't have to ask her now. I shake my head.

"I am so sorry, Honor. I am so sorry, whatever happened. It could not have been right. I hope you will accept my apology for that day, and for so much more."

Honor is quiet. I feel her listening.

"I am just going to get a breath of air in the garden. I know you have to go. Thank you for all your help today. I could not have—you helped me profoundly. Didi will pay you for these hours."

Walking outside, I feel the grass under my shoes. The air is getting cool now, and must be coming up from the Gulf, because it's laden with salt, as if the body of water is breathing. Edgar used to like to walk in the garden with me, both here in New Orleans and in Bourg-en-Bresse, all those years ago, when I was young and had my sight. I remember how happy I was to be with him on those streets and country roads in France. He made me laugh. He would carry little Josie in his arms and point out to her a shop window, a church, a swallow.

A dog barks nearby. I think of Vasco da Gama, who repaid our haphazard care of him with such protectiveness. The back garden was his special realm to keep safe. The question keeps needling me—how much would René have offered a young colored girl, our servant, to get rid of her because of whatever she had seen in our neighbors' house? Would he have thrust a dollar into her hand? Two dollars? That money would have gone a long way to help her mother. And I can well imagine how Eleanor would have interpreted that offer of hush money. If this wealthy white man were willing to pay her eleven-year-old daughter money to hush her up about his ugly affairs, how would this not continue, at a minimum? And of what might he be capable in a year or so, once Honor had grown a little older, her beauty realized? And of what might his brother, the French painter, be capable? This painter who had started to become so interested in her daughter, enough to ask her to model for him? Eleanor must have wondered how she could keep her daughter safe from this family, with its slippery boundaries. Naturally she'd send her to a safer place, well away from this house filled with white Creoles and Frenchmen. She must have felt she was saving Honor, body and soul, and indeed she may have been right.

René wouldn't have been able to bribe his oldest brother as easily, however, would he? Of course Edgar may have seen something too—René's artificial cheerfulness, maybe, or his guilty face, or the way he hesitated in the middle of the dirt road between our houses, to light a cigarette, while I was nursing my newborn. Edgar still had his sight, after all, even if it was diminished. He was no fool, either. It doesn't take actual sight to see with clarity, alas. Edgar would not have been able to toss off his brother's actions as nothing. To take his own life—I see this now—might have seemed a wiser choice than to continue in a world where his youngest brother could behave so irresponsibly, could take a mistress in a neighboring house—the good friend of his own wife, who had just given birth once more.

How disturbing it all must have seemed to Edgar, if he discovered even a fraction of this. What did Honor read in his sketchbook? *Knowledge is awful*—was that it? *How do I tell her—it is not just my sight that I'm mourning.*

I'm dismayed—shamed—now, as I recall my effort to soothe what I felt to be Edgar's anguish over his encroaching blindness. All that ardent consolation I gave to him, about how you have to make use of what you can see, no matter what! He must have listened to me incredulously, wondering how in God's name I could miss what was happening right in front of me.

Could it be so, then, that René could have had America already? Could he already have found his way into her bed, and between her legs? Could he have been doing that the very morning when I was recovering from my baby's birth? Could he have been doing that when his brother was painting Honor and the children on the doorstep? Could he have been doing that when I was nursing the baby, and comforting Josie? Could he have been doing that when I discovered Edgar bent over the washbasin, the slick mouth on his wrist? Could he have been doing that—this flood rises and spills over all my levees, into my entire being—all through that winter of Edgar's visit, and all through the years that followed—five more years, in which I welcomed my husband to our bed, and had two more babies, one of whom would die at the age of one? René claimed throughout those years to love me. And who knows, who can tell, maybe René did love me, but what is it worth, love like that?

It strikes me now, if Edgar had seen René walking across the little back street from the Oliviers' house—if he had seen him talking insistently with an eleven-year-old Honor, in her thin dress and her sandals, her pretty face, and opening his wallet—then he must have understood me to be truly blind, in more ways than one. *How can you not see what's going on, Tell?* I imagine him thinking. *Can you not sense when your own young and charming husband, my childish brother, has betrayed you? Can you not smell it on him? Can you not discover it in his kisses, or his resistance to kissing? Can you not feel it in the way he is drawn to her, like a stupid bumblebee to an open flower? Can you not gather it in the way he hovers around her when she sings? Can you not hear it in his asinine compliments to her? And can you not sense how loose he is, how dangerous even to a child, your servant? A pretty child, on the other side of the color line? If you could see her, you would understand.*

No, I cannot, I would have said then. *I have no idea what you're saying, and I wish to ask you kindly to say no more.*

So, Edgar, I think to the presence hanging, bruised and grieving, about this new house, this new garden, which—I am all too aware now—contains my history just as surely as it contains these boxes of clothes and shells and embroidered linens. *All those paintings you created. All those drawings. Did each one emerge, then, out of some love or sorrow?*

some fury or helplessness? Did you hope I would comprehend what was in those images, in spite of not being able to see them with my own eyes? Or did you hope I'd be as unaware of your art as I proved to be?

The children awash in the sand and dust of a back garden. The dog with his long pink tongue hanging out, as he does his best to guard the back gate. The gate, ajar, because the husband has already escaped to the house squatting across the ragged fence. The woman blindly arranging flowers, the world around her invisible except for the blur of light green out the window, or not even that. The woman sitting ill at ease in the chair, hemmed in by the table, her hand a claw, her eyes dark pits. The girl wrapped in a shroud-like sheet, on the sofa. The lovely woman sitting cloaked in a chair, pretending to be simply a friend who has been helping in a birth. Two women battling in a saffron room, one pleading in agony, or else rushing to accuse, the other defending herself from accusation, the man a shadow cowering at the piano.

I see it now, how Edgar was indeed holding up a mirror to our life, if only we could look into it with honesty. Easier by far to discount the messenger. Maybe I was a cousin to Eurydice after all, and it was truly Edgar who tried to rescue me. What if I didn't want to return to the world above, though, with its blue skies and green grass, if I'd have to see clearly there? In that case, it wasn't Edgar's fault. It wasn't that he looked back, like Orpheus at the threshold. It's that I turned back myself, happy enough to embrace the blank walls and my dark, disloyal king.

•

Honor has come outside to find me. I had thought she had rushed home.

She says, in an anxious voice, "*Pardon*, Madame! Would you like to come in now? Shall I fetch you some coffee?"

For one wild instant, I have the strangest sensation that Josie is here, right next to Honor. I sense her yearning for her childhood friend of the back yard. I sense her yearning to embrace me. Their lives were so different. For Josie, education, piano lessons, servants, and the knowledge of her own color cloaking and protecting her—and yet look now. Josie is dead, and here is Honor still. She has escaped to a city where she is making her own life, and her own truths.

"Thank you, Honor, no coffee," I say. "I shall come in, though. You're right. It's much colder than I'd thought."

Shadows are our thoughts made visible.

9

As I come into the house with Honor, trying to imagine how to get through the remainder of this day, the fragrance of King cakes fills the air. I know Hattie too will leave pretty soon, after putting out a cold supper for the children and me. She has been here since six this morning. A hard life, indeed. There is no justice.

I can hear Gaston playing upstairs with Pierre's old tin soldiers, and Odile talking with him.

"Excuse me, Madame. It is something else," says Honor. "Something I have found. I feel I should tell you."

"Yes?"

"I should have told you before. I meant to tell you, but I felt disturbed, and I wasn't sure what to do."

"Is it something to do with my children?" I start to walk to the staircase.

"No."

I let my breath out. "Well, then?"

"I'm sorry. It has to do with something I found. In the sketchbook."

A letter from Edgar? I think. A photograph? A picture of me, making me look like a rhinoceros? A love letter from René to America?

"It is some writing Mademoiselle Joséphine did."

"What do you mean?"

"She appears to have written—well, almost a diary—on the last page."

"Of Edgar's—of Monsieur Degas' sketchbook? You mean, right on the paper?"

"Yes, Madame."

A wet wind rising in my ribs, my heart.

"Could you read her words to me, Honor?" I say in a low voice. I cannot ask anyone else. Who else could I ask?

I sit in one of the armchairs, and I think Honor sits on the ottoman nearby. I can hear her skirts rustling, as she clears her throat.

"She writes in French," Honor begins. She clears her throat again. A vivid picture of her and Josie, as small girls, eating apricots on the doorstep, comes to me. They developed their own patois, largely indecipherable to us.

"Yes."

"Actually, it looks as if she wrote at different times. I'm not sure how to read, or where to start. I'm not sure if it is right."

"I am not sure either, Honor. But Josie is gone. Maybe she would have wanted her words to be discovered."

Honor is silent. I sense her weighing this situation, asking God, maybe, for the right thing to do.

"I have only you, Honor, to help me understand this. It's a terrible thing to ask of you."

"No, it's—."

Honor and I sit for a moment, as if perched in that same tree where she and Josie spent a whole afternoon.

"I see penciled words," she says at last, "but many have been erased. That looks like the start."

"Ah! Can you read any of those words?"

I wait while Honor appears to study Josie's markings.

"*Non*, Madame. Well, maybe one. It looks like—."

Honor stops.

"Go on."

"I'm not sure, Madame, but in truth it looks like the word Honor."

"Honor?"

"Possibly."

I can just feel Josie's heat, that day on my bed, once her baby sister had been born. I can just feel her warm forehead, as I smoothed her hair. "She tore it," Josie said, meaning the sketch, but soon after that she said something so startling. "I hate your husband"—could she really have said that to me? Washing her mouth out with soap would have been senseless, though, and I'm glad I didn't do it that day. She was only telling the truth, after all.

"Then here's a date: March 21st, 1873."

"1873, in March?"

Josie was ten years old then. Edgar sailed back to France that March.

"Go on," I say, trying my best to brace myself.

"Mademoiselle Joséphine wrote: '*Cher cousin*—but that's scratched out. Then *Chère Honor*—but that is scratched out too. Then it's '*Dear Sketchbook, I think I should show you to Maman. You are mine now though. Cousin Edgar left you here.*'"

Honor pauses. "Should I go on?"

I nod. "It would be a great kindness. Thank you."

I think for the tenth time that Honor will say she can't manage it, but then she starts to read again—courageously, movingly.

"'*Maman was happy with Cousin Edgar here and now she is sad again. He took the train two weeks ago and she says soon he will be in Paris so far away. I'm going to keep you close and hide you in my chest with the key with my best things so you aren't discovered and shipped back to him because then I won't have anything to remember my cousin Edgar by and he is a good man, he's a great artist and he had hard times too I know this is very true anyone could know it from just looking at his face, so sad. He loved Maman of this I am sure!'"*

Honor stops. I am besieged by Josie's words. I had not known she could have seen things this way. How did she get such a notion about Edgar? My daughter.

"Go on," I say, my face burning. "It's all right. What can it matter now?"

"'I am more sure of it than of my own name.'"

Josie! I cry out to the spirit leaning in to me. *Why didn't you ever talk to me about Edgar, after that winter? Why didn't you tell me how much you cared about him, how sorry you were to see him go?* I think with a terrible pinch of sorrow how homesick she became a year later, too, when she went to the Catholic boarding school. Maybe the sketchbook became her companion, because it had been Edgar's, and he'd shown her love. He'd drawn her and painted her, just as he had drawn and painted Honor.

"'I posed for him standing by the back door and then when the doctor came to fix my foot. Cousin Edgar wrapped a sheet around me and draped another sheet over the chair and he made me laugh when he painted me I almost forgot the pain of my big toe having to be cut into by M. Hâche—my cousin gave me a peppermint from his pocket and then I fell asleep after the doctor had done the most painful part. I liked the painting very much and I want to write to my cousin to tell him so though I did look a little funny wrapped up like a mummy but that's all right, I think I looked older than my own age ten. He wanted to get the colors just right he said. He said I was a good model and very patient I wonder if I will ever see that painting again,

Cousin Edgar took all of his canvases with him.'"

I keenly wish now, more than ever before, that I could have set eyes on that painting of Josie wrapped up in a big white sheet on the daybed in my bedroom. The podiatrist had come to repair an ingrown toenail. Edgar must have painted the picture in the late winter some time. Josie looked half asleep in the finished version, apparently. Mouche said the girl in the painting could almost have breathed her last breath, except for the shine of her hair and something about the comfort of her pose. I'm soothed myself for a moment, hearing this detail in Josie's words, of the peppermint Edgar gave to her. Maybe the peppermint and the podiatrist's gentle attentions to her feet after he'd done the cutting helped her fall asleep. I remember Didi had to pay the doctor extra to stay for an hour beyond his appointment, so that Edgar could draw him.

Mouche said, about that painting, "Well, it would be nice if Edgar could show your Josie in a beautiful dress, sitting in the garden with her cousins, or reading a book. I don't know, Tell. Edgar is deep! And I don't know why he placed that ugly bathing tub beside her. He likes such odd things."

I could answer Mouche now, although I'm not sure she'd like my answer. Because it hits me, how Edgar might have been thinking how Josie was only ten, comforted by a peppermint, but soon she'd be older. Soon she would be a young woman, bathing. She would take off her clothes, and step into her new life, with a husband of her own. And what would her life be like? Edgar might have worried. Could she grow blind, like her mother? Could she marry someone who would carry on affairs over backyard fences?

Could she pose for a painter eager to gaze his fill at her body, all her curves, as Edgar gazes at so many women who must pose naked for him?

Or maybe Edgar was simply showing worry for his young cousin's health, for her life, as if he could see how she would fall ill one April day, three years after her stepfather left. Maybe Edgar could imagine how she would try to talk to me at the end, but the words could not form, overwhelmed as she was in fever and pain, as I tried to bathe her. My daughter, my bird, my poem.

Honor is saying now, "That is what Mademoiselle Joséphine wrote that day. Then—here's another part, just underneath, in pen. Should I read this too?"

I nod.

"*'Honor has gone, and I am sure she will never come here again.'*" Honor's voice slows here. She sounds far away.

"*'Thank you, dear Sketchbook, for having pictures of her. It's my fault she left. It's not all my fault, perhaps, but I felt jealous of her having the drawing, I felt jealous Cousin Edgar drew her and she looked* si belle, *I wished he'd drawn me really my face too not just from a distance where I had the hat on covering my face. Honor was happy to have that sketch, and I was angry at her. I'm sorry I tore it. If I could write to her.'*"

Again Honor pauses. If she cannot read further, it will have to be all right.

"*'If I could write to her, I would tell her I'm sorry.'*"

All I can see is young Josie, writing this secretly in Edgar's sketchbook. So much she must have held inside— guilt and love and an unarticulated bond with Honor torn in half—right up to her last difficult breaths, when she lay fevered and distraught. Eighteen years old, her future cut off entirely in that labored rising and falling of her chest.

"Then here's another part, in a blue ink. By the handwriting, Mademoiselle Joséphine looks to have been older. She's written this on the very last page, a fresh page. Oh, here's a date too, written very small: *le 24 avril 1878.*"

The day after René left. Josie held my hand that day. She persuaded me to go back to bed, and she brought me tea. She'd found me weeping on the floor of my bedroom. How the daughter becomes the mother!

"'*I come back to you now, dear Sketchbook, and possibly this will be my last time, for I am aware that I should not hold on to Cousin Edgar's drawings all my life. He'll want them, even if he decides one day to do away with them, because of the memories they cause to rise up in him, as they cause memories to rise up in me.*

"'*Before I send this precious book to him, filled with so much that I've loved, I will have to cut out this sheet, with my silly childhood writings on one side, and this on the other.*

"'*In abandoning my mother and all of us yesterday, in this scandal of his creation, M. René De Gas has shown the world what he is made of. I can't be glad of it. I would have rather seen him die. He could have been killed in a duel for all I care. I would have done anything to protect my mother from this knowledge about this person she married and had five children with. I am, alas, not surprised at this ugly and embarrassing affair he's been conducting for so many years.*'"

Honor is quiet.

"It is simply history now," I say to her. "And I believe—I trust—that you and I both owe this to Joséphine, to listen to her words. I have no other way to hear her." I pause, and go on. "I have experienced much in my life. This is hard for me, yes, and for you too, I imagine, but I feel that after today this can be just a memory for us both, Honor. No one else will have to see what Josie wrote here. It's just, I have to listen once to every word."

"Yes," Honor says. After a long minute, she starts to read again. Her voice is so subdued, I have to work hard to hear her.

"*I'm only surprised that he actually made such a brutal move, as to flee with his mistress without one word or kiss for Maman or for any of my siblings. From the first day I knew, when I saw him shaking Honor's shoulder and trying to give her something from his wallet, which she pushed away, I knew he did not love Maman anymore, not as his only love. My knowledge was confirmed so many times, as I grew older. I am fifteen years old now, and I know more of the world, but when I was a child I thought the earth had turned upside down, and inside out, to think that my mother's husband could have an affair for so many years, with the woman I cannot name. The day I caught them kissing in the hallway, during a Mardi Gras party. The day I saw their hands touch when* she *pretended to be looking for some sheet music on the piano. The day, at dusk, when I saw him walking out of her back door, Vasco da Gama barking at him. No wonder M. René De Gas wanted me gone. And I was glad to be gone away to school, if only to escape his artifice and lies, yet I missed my mother achingly.*

"'*I will cut this sheet out soon, because I do not want anyone—anyone!—to find it. Yet in writing this here, I feel closer to the creator of these images, my cousin Edgar, who looked at me with sudden tenderness on so many days. It is not for myself I grieve, however—it is for Maman, who has a soul of such goodness, she can't see other people's faults.*

"'*Well, now, hélas, she has been forced to see. She's been keeping to her room since he left. Vasco da Gama has more courage and nobility than such a man could ever have."'*

Honor's voice has grown so soft, she is almost murmuring.

"'And one day Maman may know this too, that she's freer without this person. I hope the knowledge is a consolation. I hope she does not feel she should have known. She upheld her part in her marriage, by heaven. I love her with all my heart, and may I never in my life cause her such sorrow as he has done.'"

"Is there anything more?"

"Just one more part. It's at the bottom of that page, in pencil. It looks as if Mademoiselle Joséphine wrote it in a shaky hand."

I think I know what is coming. "Go on."

"'April __ 1881. If I die of this fever, whoever finds this writing, please cut it out from M. Edgar Degas' sketchbook and mail the sketchbook to him. Please burn these pages upon which I wrote, in my childishness. And please forgive me. Yours in honor, Mlle. Estelle Joséphine Balfour.'"

10

The day has fled. Honor says gently, "I must go, Madame." She rises and stands in front of me.

I rise too. I put out my hands and touch Honor's shoulders. So young she is! Her shoulders feel light but strong.

"I cannot thank you sufficiently," I say.

Around us I can just hear our old household, up on Esplanade, with the parrot chattering, the dog galloping past, the children playing a game of spelling bee or cards. A young Honor is here, holding little Odile. A young Josie is reading on the back stoop, in the dusk. Edgar is painting someone—Mouche, maybe, or me.

I hear Honor walk into the kitchen. As she says goodbye to Hattie, and opens the back door to go, I imagine her bringing the fragrance of the King cakes with her as she goes down the steps and catches the tram up Esplanade, then walks the few blocks to her mother's house. I picture her as a child running home that day in December, ten years ago, frightened after fetching her things. I picture her telling her mother Eleanor, and Eleanor's face as she comprehends the risk her daughter is in, if she stays on with us. I think of all Honor must have seen in our household: babies being born, a woman losing her sight, a husband in the wrong house, a drawing made especially of her, but thrown in the trash, a white girl—younger than Honor, once her companion, although never her equal—who felt privileged to grab at the sketch and make it tear.

Now Odile and Gaston are sitting at the big oak table in the kitchen, eating toast and soup, and the cold chicken Hattie has prepared for them.

"I did see gold, though, Odile," Gaston is saying, retelling the treasure hunt that has occupied his day. "You can see for yourself. But I had to cover it up again, so no one would find it tonight."

"I doubt that anyone is going to come looking for gold right here on Esplanade Avenue, Gaston," Odile says.

"They might."

"Yes, they might, and I might grow wings tonight in my bed."

"That's silly," says Gaston.

"Hattie," I say, "you may go now. I'm sure you're eager to get home. It's been a long day."

"Yes, Madame. I will go on now."

I picture Hattie taking the tram, just as Honor has. And I picture Honor on the train in a few days, buoyed by her mother's love, sad to go, and yet eager to return to her own life in Washington. What will she paint next? Whom will she love? How will she remember this day, these hours cut out of time? Will she carry something of Josie with her? Or will she be glad to erase her, to erase all of us? What apology is great enough?

And how would I open up even to Didi, after all these years, about René? I don't want to discover that she knew about his affair all along, as Josie did—knew that it hadn't been simply at the end, but ongoing year after year. I would be devastated to discover that Mouche knew too. Were they wishing to protect me? Am I glad if they did? I don't know,

I just don't. And I don't want to bring up this subject again, ever. I only hope that one day—one bright day—I will be able to open the window inside me, and let all these pests, these crawling bugs and flying insects, these stinkbugs and snakes, leave, just leave my house and my soul, and let me be at peace. I am glad my marriage is over. I am glad to know I will never marry again.

"You can only find the gold in moonlight, though," Gaston is saying. He's talking again with his mouth full.

"Why is that, Gaston?" I don't hear too much irony in Odile's voice. Sometimes she can suddenly become indulgent with Gaston, instead of arguing with him, a blessed relief. It is in moments like this that I know she is growing up. One day she may have children of her own.

"Because it's fairy gold, probably."

"You mean it isn't real?" asks Odile.

"Yes, it's real," says Gaston. "It's magical. Of course it's real."

•

"I have to find a way to sell my work," Edgar said to me one day—it must have been some time in the latter half of January, that winter.

"You *have* been selling your work, though, haven't you?" I asked.

I could feel him looking intently at me.

"Well, if you could call it selling. I've sold a couple of paintings this year, Tell, but it's impossible. I'm still waiting to hear about those two oils I left with my dealer. What's the matter with this world? Good art goes begging, and all the while people lust after what's easier, or more pleasing. People only want what's pretty."

In a moment, he added in a fervent voice, "I can only do the art I do, Tell. Can you understand that? I can only see what I see. I can't paint something superficial, or some local color, just to sell it. I'd rather cut my wrists properly and be done with the whole inane business."

"Stop."

"I'm not threatening to do that. I was wrong, to try that. You were right. But what I'm saying is, I hope you of all people, Tell, can see what I'm trying to do in my art. I'm trying to do something large, something significant. The world is filled with hard things. It needs an art that can show it in all its brutality."

"I wish I *could* see, Edgar! But I think I do know something of your art, what you're trying to do in it. I wish I could understand you better, though."

"Am I so difficult to understand, Tell?"

I sensed something so deep in the way he asked that question. I felt inexpressible tenderness in him, and sorrow, and something else I could not define.

"Yes," I said, trying to smile. "Yes, you are."

•

As I half-listen to Odile and Gaston talking, the question shakes me to my foundation: had Edgar been in love with me, then? Is this one reason he hovered around me, so sober and so wounded? Could this be why he opened his wrist in despair? I have to recognize, the thought occurred to me more than once that winter, especially after that day of his bloody attempt. I had to push it away, though. How could I have responded to him in any other way? And I didn't wound him, in any case, did I? At least, I had no intention of that. I was like a swimmer just trying to stay on course, through blooms of jellyfish or cold salt waves in my face. I was just trying to continue on, with the life I'd chosen. Did Edgar watch me from his own leaky raft? Did he wish he could pull me on board, have me give up that effort? Yet he couldn't wish that. His brother was my husband. He had to just hope I could keep swimming, blindly and in good faith, like a dog.

"Have you heard about Edgar's new painting?" Mouche asked me one day. It must have been some time before Mardi Gras, maybe in early February, because she was sewing costumes, one for her husband William and one for René. She had set me to doing the hems. René was going as some kind of bug in the Crewe parade. Our house had started to fill with the usual excitement and flurry over the upcoming festivities, in spite of the troubles buzzing around us, and in spite of Edgar's evident unhappiness.

"A new painting?"

"William's in it," Mouche said proudly. "And Papa. And René. Edgar used some drawings he'd done of Papa's cotton office, before Christmas, I gather, and now he's been drawing a lot of people to go into a painting. He's hoping to sell it to some wealthy English mill-owner, or at least that's what William says. He even put in Papa's old partners. He says Monsieur Livaudais is in a sketch, standing up at a high desk, looking over accounts. And the picture shows William offering a handful of cotton to some buyer."

"What's René doing?"

"I don't know. I'm glad, though, that Edgar's finally talking about painting a picture that will sell."

René felt strongly enough about this painting of the cotton office to complain to me about it. He found me one afternoon walking up and down our bedroom with the baby in my arms, trying to lull her to sleep for her nap.

"That painting is awful. I mean, it's well painted—Edgar is brilliant, and at his best—but it makes us look idle," he said. "Or, it makes *me* look idle. Do you know what I'm doing in it, Tell?"

"I can't think."

"I'm sitting smack in the center, lolling in a chair, with my legs out, and a cigarette in my mouth, reading the newspaper, as if I have no work to do at all! Is that what Edgar thinks of me?"

"Well, René, you posed for him. You must have known what you'd look like."

"I posed for him, but I didn't know what the thing would look like, once he had the painting underway. He just told me to sit and read the paper as I always do, and I didn't think about it twice. It just looks ridiculous, to be sitting in the middle of a cotton office that's supposed to be orderly and busy, and to be reading a damned paper."

"It's art, though, René. It isn't trying to show any truth about you as an actual person. You're just a cheap model for Edgar!" I smiled, trying to win a laugh and a kiss. I added, lightly, "Look at all the paintings Edgar has done of me! You don't see me complaining about any of it. Mouche says I look as if my hands have turned into claws in one of them! Your brother has a good imagination, that's all I can say."

I couldn't say more, about Edgar, and what he'd been suffering. René could see for himself, if he chose to. I am sure I could have listened more carefully to the warnings Edgar folded into his images of the cotton office. All I wanted to do, though, was help to repair the rift between them. Heaven have mercy on me for my stupidity.

"It's worse than that, though, Tell. This picture is demeaning. Edgar put your father right in the front, sitting in a comfortable chair, pulling the staple of a piece of cotton, like a simpleton. It makes his work look like nothing. The only one who's really looking earnest is John Livaudais, who's hunched over a big accounting book. And do you know, Tell," René said, his voice thick with emotion, "what Edgar has put right in the front right corner of the thing?"

"Shh, the baby."

Jeanne had just fallen asleep, her weight relaxed in my arms. I lay her in her bassinet and smoothed her fine wisps of hair.

"A wastebasket." He gave an insulted snort. "He put a wastebasket right in the front of the picture! Filled with what look to be bills! How do you like that? What in Christ's name is he doing? Is he making fun of your father and me, William, the whole lot of us? Is he referring to your father's bankruptcy? It's an insult."

"Calm yourself," I said, although I had started to feel alarmed at this description. "Why should you jump to that conclusion? Don't cotton offices have wastebaskets in them?"

I sat on our bed. I could hear René pacing around

the room, from the window to the door and back again. I wished we could go back to his arrival in New Orleans with Edgar, and start over again. And maybe, in some part of my heart, I wished we could go back to France, before I permitted myself to fall in love with this handsome cousin, this lovely boy with dreams and ambition, so quick to find his way in to a woman's heart and body. He had seemed untethered then, and I'd thought I could tether him, bind him to me with my own beauty and power.

"It's a slap in the face, Tell. Your father's business goes bankrupt, and mine runs into trouble, and Edgar paints us sitting in chairs reading newspapers and daydreaming, while John Livaudais sweats over the books? Just behind the trash? You tell me if this has no personal message in it from Edgar to me, or to your father."

I wished René could stop being so agitated, yet I started to realize how indeed that painting could be a slap in the face. René had created the mound of debt we would never be able to repay. And I realize even more keenly, now, how much René threw away.

"I can understand, my love," I said that day. "Your business means a lot to you. But why do you have to think Edgar is folding in some personal message about you in his painting? He wants to make it good enough to sell at a high price." I added, "You know he's been very patient and kind to us this winter."

"I know. He's done his best. And I've always looked up to him. He's been a good brother. In these last few weeks, though, something has changed. His stupid paintings! None of them are flattering! Don't you agree? And in any case, he's so morose. I can't stand having him here, skulking around. If I could pack his bags for him today, and get him on a train to Mobile, I would do it."

Something in René's tone might have alerted me, but it didn't, or at least it alerted me only to René's distress about Edgar. I wished I could tell him how distressed Edgar too had been—enough to take his own life—but I hesitated to do that. Somehow I sensed that René would be even less sympathetic toward Edgar, if he knew.

"I hadn't realized his presence was so difficult for you, René. You've been his defender, more than anything, all winter, at least you seemed that way at first."

"Yes, well, Edgar can defend himself. I'm tired of doing him that service."

"I thought you've been happy having Edgar here, most of the time. And I thought you felt sympathy for him."

René sighed heavily, and I could just picture him running his hand through his thick hair.

"I have felt some sympathy. His paintings are good, even though they're strange, and they should find buyers. Sometimes I think his paintings are works of genius. I've felt other things too, though. I *feel* other things. He's a very hard person to have around. You have to admit that."

I had, in fact, been glad that Edgar had started to do some of his sketching and painting in the city. He'd had the use of a small space at René's office, to work on his pictures of cotton merchants.

"I do admit it," I said. "But Edgar cares about you very much, René."

René came closer to me, and then he sat on the bed and held my hand for a moment. I loved to have his hand in mine, even if just for that instant. I thought it might help him, if he could remember how much he had with me, with our children—how lucky he was.

Before I could say anything soothing, though, he stood up again, and I could tell he was walking toward the door to the hall. I could picture him standing with his hand on the knob, as he looked back at me.

"It's terrible to sense him always watching us, though, Tell. It's too close quarters. I can't breathe in my house, or light a cigarette, or sneeze, or—anything, truly—without Edgar noticing. Don't you feel that?"

Did I? I wasn't sure.

"I feel him to be lonely, and in pain," I said, thinking of his wrist. "That's all."

"Well, it's lonely people one has to watch out for," René said. "People in pain. Especially if they're your relatives."

"In any case," I said, "Edgar will be gone soon enough. He's reserved passage on a ship leaving from Havana in early March. You know that."

"I'll be sure of it when I see his train pull out of the station, and then when I hear that his ship did truly set off for France, and he can't possibly swim his way back."

René opened the door then. I listened to his hasty step on the stairs, and soon I heard the French doors at the back of the hallway open and close as he went into the back garden.

11

Edgar's painting of the song rehearsal was the last straw with René.

"What a pathetic picture that is, Tell."

He had found me walking with the baby in the front garden early one morning, and I continued to walk slowly up and down the front walk with him.

"I think the painting sounds wonderfully theatrical, René. You know Edgar loves opera. I do too. I've missed it this winter, with the opera closed."

"You're missing the point, Tell. I know you can't see the painting. Let me assure you, he's made a mockery of us again in it, only this time it's worse. It's like the duet for two cats, that silly piece children love. You know, where the two women sound like cats quarreling. *Miaou*."

I had to laugh a little at René's rendition. Luckily, this time he kept his voice low, because Edgar's room was nearby, in the front of the house.

"Is it like that?" I said, smiling, and slipping one of my arms through René's, as I held Jeanne with the other. "So it looks humorous, then? Mouche and Didi made it sound more tragic."

"It's a melodrama. One woman quarrelling with another. And he stuck me in the corner, the same color as the piano. I look like a mistake."

I moved baby Jeanne to my other shoulder. I loved how heavy her little head was, when she was asleep. The birds were making a racket, as the sun rose, and the rosemary bush near the walk had a delicious scent.

I'd been sad by then, realizing Edgar would be gone so soon. Even though I could well imagine how much lighter our house would feel, once Edgar was gone, I knew I would miss him. He'd been close by; he'd made us all into characters in his art; he'd looked at us with keen vision and, I was sure, with love.

•

"I set up the soldiers on the dresser, did you see, Maman?" Gaston is pulling on his nightshirt, in the bedroom he shares with Odile.

"Ah! You must have a regular war going on there."

"I'm reading about the Three Kings tonight, am I not, Maman?" Odile asks. "For Epiphany."

"Yes, the Three Kings." I slip my hand down Odile's arm, to feel the Bible on her lap, on top of the covers. I would know its soft and nubbly leather binding anywhere, and the smooth paper edges, which must still be gold. Maman gave me this Bible when I married René, and I always wondered if she'd been so worried about me, she'd hoped this gift might add its protection. One day before she died, she told me to stay strong and to hold on to my courage. "Of course I will," I assured her. "Life is not easy," she said. "We must all live with the choices we've made. I wish you the strength to live as well as you can."

"Ready?"

"*Oui*, Maman."

"*Viens ici*, Gaston."

Gaston flies into the bed with Odile, jiggling us, as I settle myself on her other side, my arm around her. She's in a flannel nightgown she found in one of the boxes today, probably one of Josie's favorites: her white one or her pink one with sprigs of roses all over it.

I gather that Odile has forgotten all about Edgar's sketchbook and Honor's visit, amid the excitement of the day, the parrot in the trees, the piano arriving, the stray cat, the King cakes baking. In the morning, she'll help me plan for our party tomorrow afternoon with her cousins. Why should she care about those drawings of ten years ago? She has no memory of Edgar, so how could she care about him? Gaston too must have his head filled with visions of fairy gold and the cat who even now is asleep right outside our back door, on the blanket Gaston put out for it, its belly full of the warm milk Odile heated up herself and poured into a little saucer. Maybe it will grow to be a good mouser.

As Odile finds the story in *Matthew*, and begins, I imagine Edgar here with us, listening too, waiting until he has my full attention. Josie loved this story of the Wise Men. She made a picture, the winter Edgar was here, of those kings, walking with a camel under a starlit sky. I wonder if that picture can be found in the boxes still waiting downstairs. I will have to ask Odile to look tomorrow.

"'Now when Jesus was born in Bethlehem of Judaea in the days of Herod the king, behold, there came wise men from the east to Jerusalem, saying, Where is He that is born King of the Jews? For we have seen His Star in the east, and are come to worship Him.'"

I listen to the story of Herod, commanding the wise

men to find the new king, and to come back and tell him of this king's whereabouts. What a liar and a betrayer Herod was, saying he only wished to worship the new king. I wonder if Odile understands.

"'When they had heard the king, they departed; and lo, the Star, which they saw in the east, went before them, till it came and stood over where the young Child was.'"

"Can stars do that?" asks Gaston.

"What?"

"Move in the sky, ahead of you?"

"Well, this one did," says Odile. "It was a special star, anyhow."

"I don't think it was a star, really," says Gaston, starting to sound sleepy. "I think it was God."

"Well, just listen. 'When they saw the Star, they rejoiced with exceeding great joy. And when they were come into the house—'"

"I thought it was a stable."

"This time it says house, Gaston. 'When they were come into the house, they saw the young Child with Mary His mother, and fell down, and worshipped Him: and when they had opened their treasures, they presented unto Him gifts; gold, and frankincense, and myrrh.'"

"What's myrrh, Odile?"

"Something precious. Just listen, Gaston, or else I won't read to you again." She gives a theatrical sigh, and continues, "'And being warned of God in a dream that they should not return to Herod, they departed into their own country another way.'"

"They dreamed God said that?" asks Gaston.

"Yes. God warned them in a dream."

"God came into their dream?"

"It says so."

"I think that's the best place to stop, Odile." I don't want her to go into the last part of the story, the slaughter of the innocents.

"It goes on, though, Maman."

"The last part isn't so pretty, and in any case I like the ending you've just read. Does it go, 'they departed into their own country *on their own*?'"

"'*Some other way.*'"

"Ah," I say, thinking of Edgar saying goodbye to me, in the hallway, before he caught the train at long last, one day that March. "I wonder what the wise men's own country was like."

"Probably filled with jewels," says Gaston.

"And camels," says Odile. "And everyone had lots of food and nice clothes, and cakes."

"And books, if they're so wise," I say.

"Maybe they'd have King cakes every day," says Gaston dreamily.

As I kiss my children goodnight, I think how clear it is, to the kings, that they've come upon precisely what they sought. They followed a star, and it led them to a baby. And then God came to them in a dream—as if they all dreamed the same dream!—and they knew to avoid the betrayer, and go home some other way.

Could it have been so clear, though, what those kings thought they'd seen? Did they understand they'd been privileged to witness something sacred? And why did they think gold or frankincense or myrrh would be the right gifts? What would Christ ever do with such wealth, when

He was after wealth of spirit only? It's a strange story, when you think about it. How often people mistake what's right in front of them. How often we think we see clearly, and yet it's all fuzzy, really, what is before us.

•

Because what did Edgar say to me, finally? I try to remember as I close the children's bedroom door and make my way down the stairs.

"You matter to me more than anyone, *tu sais*." Is that what he said? "Whatever happens, Tell, I hope you know this."

"What will happen, Edgar?" I asked, trying to make light of his odd, ravaged tone, and yet I felt shaken. I did not want him to go. I stood in the hallway with him, his bags packed, the baby in my arms. He'd been looking all over the house for his sketchbook, but the house was a mess, and he couldn't find it anywhere.

Edgar stood close to me and held my elbow.

"Anything, Tell. Anything can happen in life, can't it? Just know that I stood here beside you, on this March morning, and wished you well. Just know that I have tried my best."

"What are you talking about, dearest cousin?" I asked, trying to laugh, but he still held my elbow, and I sensed him so close to me. I said, "I will remember, Edgar. Thank you for your good wishes."

Did I feel a shiver pass lightly along my spine or through my heart? Did I wonder about the love held for me by my husband or my neighbor?

I missed Edgar already, and he was right in front of me. I had the incomprehensible urge to gather my children up and have us all walk out the door with him.

Before Edgar and I could say one more word, however, René had come into the hallway from the back garden and had started to help Edgar carry his bags to the neighbors' carriage we'd borrowed. The children had been alerted, and were jumping all around Edgar, shouting their adieus.

"Ready?" René asked, jovial now that Edgar was about to go.

"May I see you all again," Edgar murmured to me. "Send the sketchbook along, if you discover it, Tell. It contains my life here. It's very important to me."

I felt like throwing my arms around him. I felt like pleading with him to stay.

"I will," I said.

He kissed me on both cheeks.

"My love stays with you," he said, and he was off.

12

Glad for the two children sleeping upstairs, I bend to touch the ottoman I sat on earlier in the day, and then the couch, looking for Edgar's sketchbook. At last I find it on the mantel. Opening it, touching the paper, I wish I could hear all of Edgar's words again. Maybe I would understand them this time. Could I ask Odile to read them to me tomorrow? *Hélas,* no. Never could I ask my child such a thing. Honor was the only reader I could trust profoundly—I realize this in full force now. She was the only reader who could understand. I wonder if she too yearns to see this sketchbook again, for her own reasons.

What were the last words, which seemed so puzzling when Honor read them? Something about Havana—something about going home. *The rest of one's life. Here is love.* Was that it? Something "terrible," then. And somewhere, that word "alters."

Love is not love, which alters.

And it's now that it strikes me head on, the great blow: what Edgar must have known, and what I was blind to. I try to brush the thought aside, push it aside, but it keeps coming back, worrying me, clinging to me. For I realize, in this quiet house in New Orleans, on the verge of Epiphany, that if only I could let the thought in, I would have to acknowledge that I loved Edgar as much as he loved me. Sober, difficult, bruised, yearning, agonized, impossible, troubled Edgar. Honorable Edgar. If I had recognized my love for him then, what could I have done with the knowledge? To recognize it now—well, it is too late by half a lifetime.

I hold the sketchbook close as I sit in an armchair. How great my mistakes have been. And yet if I had not married René, I would not have had the five children I was graced with. I would not have the two remaining, asleep upstairs right now. If you could only have a larger view—if you could only see from the angle and serenity of heaven—you might be able to understand why things go as they do. Maman was right. It takes courage to live.

After contemplating all this for a long time, I come up with the simplest plan. It is insufficient, but it will have to do. I will ask Hattie to cut out Josie's words tomorrow, so that I can hold them safe here. I cannot imagine burning that paper, in spite of Josie's wishes, although one day I might manage it.

I will also ask Hattie to cut out one or two of the best sketches of Honor, and to make sure to give them to her before she goes back to Washington. I will ask her to place them between a few layers of fresh, clean paper, so they will be protected. I will write Honor a note, saying, "These are for you, and of you. Please take them, with my blessing and in memory of Mlle. Joséphine, who sat with you one day in a tree high above us all. In gratitude, and with sincere good wishes, Madame Estelle Musson."

Then—I am sure of it—I will wrap the sketchbook and ask Didi to mail it to Edgar across the ocean. I'll write a letter that will let him know I understand something of what he went through that winter—what he may have carried with him all this time. I will tell him it's all right.

What's happened has happened. It's all in the past, and none of it was his fault. He couldn't have helped more than he did. I'll say I hope his art is selling like hot cakes. I will describe this house to him. I will describe Odile, and Gaston, and the new words our parrot Persie has come up with. I will say that whatever else the world has wrought, something of love remains. I think I will do this. Surely I will.

About the author

Harriet Scott Chessman is the author of the acclaimed novels *The Beauty of Ordinary Things* (2013), *Someone Not Really Her Mother* (a 2004 *San Francisco Chronicle* Best Book, and a *Good Morning America* Book Club Choice), *Lydia Cassatt Reading the Morning Paper* (2001), and *Ohio Angels* (1999). She is also the author of the libretto for *My Lai,* a contemporary operatic piece commissioned by Kronos Performing Arts Association in 2015. She has taught literature and creative writing at Yale University, Bread Loaf School of English, and Stanford University's Continuing Studies Program. She lives in Guilford, Connecticut.

Acknowledgments

I have gained valuable information about the American period of Edgar Degas' life from *Degas and New Orleans: A French Impressionist in America*, which accompanied the 1999 exhibition organized by the New Orleans Museum of Art, together with Ordrupgaard Museum. Edited by Gail Feigenbaum, then Curator of Painting at the New Orleans Museum of Art, this catalogue is filled with superb essays by Gail Feigenbaum, Christopher Benfey, Christina Vella, Marilyn R. Brown, and Jean Sutherland Boggs.

Among the many other scholarly works helpful to me in my research, I wish especially to acknowledge Christopher Benfey's fascinating *Degas in New Orleans: Encounters in the Creole World of Kate Chopin and George Washington Cable* and Henri Loyrette's *Degas: Passion and Intellect* (translated by I. Mark Paris).

Degas: Letters, edited by Marcel Guérin and translated by Marguerite Kay, has been an excellent resource, as have the two volumes of *The Notebooks of Edgar Degas*, edited by Theodore Reff.

In addition, I could not have completed this novel without the help of wonderful readers.

First of all, I owe so much to Jon Roemer for welcoming this novel to Outpost19, and for editing it with grace, clarity and wisdom. I am grateful to the whole Outpost19 team, for a beautiful book design, copy editing, and much more.

Thank you to Maud Carol Markson for her engaged, intelligent readings of early and wildly divergent drafts, and to Jonathan Strong and Scott Elledge for so generously responding to an early version of this story with acumen and illumination.

I offer heartfelt thanks to Priscilla Gilman for her belief in this novel from its origins, and her splendid suggestions for development.

Thank you too to McCord Clayton for his vital and timely help with my first chapter, and to Helen Patton for our conversations about Edgar Degas and his American cousins, in the context of Franco-American cultural exchange.

And a big thank you to Johann Le Guelte for his careful and insightful help with the French language. All mistakes remain my own!

In a larger way, I am deeply, infinitely grateful to all of the beloved friends and family members who have buoyed me up, as a writer, throughout this long wrestling. I wish to give special thanks to Mother Abbess Lucia Kuppens, O.S.B., Mother Angèle Arbib, O.S.B., Mother Noella Marcellino, O.S.B., Mother Augusta Collins, O.S.B., Mother Margaret Georgina Patton, O.S.B., and the Community of the Abbey of Regina Laudis, for their vision, understanding, and sustaining presence.

Finally, I owe more than I can say to my children Marissa, Micah, and Gabe Wolf, and my son-in-law Tom Toro, for their love and encouragement, and their inspiring and imaginative responses to this story, in all its incarnations.

And I have benefited immensely from the brilliance and insight of Bryan J. Wolf, with whom I am always in conversation. His passionate love of art and literature, his profound love of family, and his compassion for humanity inspire me daily.